Love Stories

Love Stories

Katherine Villyard

Published in the United States by Katherine Villyard
ISBN 979-8-9868330-1-9.

"Grandfather Paradox" was originally published in *Electric Velocipede*, issue #17/18, Spring 2009, and reprinted in *Escape Pod*, March 10, 2011.

"In the Water" originally appeared in *Fictitious Force*, issue #6, 2009, and was reprinted in *Escape Pod*, May 13, 2011.

"La Divinia Commedia" originally appeared in *ChiZine*, October 2011, reprinted in *Broad Spectrum: The 2012 Broad Universe Fiction Sampler (October 30, 2012)*.

"Minotaur" appeared in *Alien Abduction: Short Fiction on the Themes of Alien and Abduction*, September 28, 2015.

"Ondine's Curse" appeared in *Electric Velocipede*, December 11, 2013

"Saving Alan Idle" appeared in *Escape Pod*, July 5, 2013.

"Underworld" appeared in *Fantastic Stories of the Imagination*, January 2015.

Contents

Love Stories

Book of Shadows

When I got home, I found a statement from my retirement account in the mailbox and an eviction notice taped to my front door. I tore open the account statement. My IRA was worth nothing. I shouldn't have invested in my company's stock. I crumpled it up and opened the door.

Inside, everything I owned was in boxes. I'd sold my sofa and TV. I'd sold most of my books to the used bookstore. I supposed I could have another garage sale and sell the bookshelves and kitchen stuff, but the eviction notice said I had a week so I'd better hurry. Mom didn't have the money, and I'd cut up my credit card when they jacked up the interest to 29%. No U-Haul for me. Maybe I should abandon all this crap and drive to Mom's, if I raised money for gas.

I wouldn't abandon my computer or my father's Book of Shadows. I couldn't do contracts without the computer, and I wasn't going anywhere without my father's book. I opened it. Inside: spells in my father's handwriting, the sum of his magical life. It even contained the spell they used to conceive me. I turned to the page on fast money.

"Hail, Habondia, Lady of Plenty," I began. I felt a sudden surge of grief for my father, but took a deep breath and went on. There were words of power, and I spoke them, calling Her to me.

It's important to visualize during a spell. I tried to remember when I felt prosperous; the measure of my success.

My Daddy's pride in me. That was what always made me feel successful. I'd never feel that again. He was dead.

As the spell demanded, I took out my last twenty dollars and burned it on the stove. It was just as well; spells that demanded a trade were more reliable that the spells that asked for something without giving something in return. Those relied on luck, and I had little or none to spare.

My father died a little over two years ago. Everyone told me things would get better. Ha. He was the one who believed in me. He was the one who taught me magic. When I earned my degree in computer science, he was the one who never doubted me for a moment.

That was before the cancer.

Great workings often shorten the lives of magicians. He never told me what he had done, what had been worth giving up part of his life. What had been worth the cancer eating his bone marrow, the dark magic of chemotherapy that had robbed him of his thick black hair? The change to his tastebuds so only ice cream, popsicles, and cotton candy tasted good that had been in exchange for a few months before the cancer had won?

Had the cancer itself been a price? And which would be worse, the cancer being meaningless or the cancer being the price he paid for something else?

The phone rang. I answered.

"Honey?" my mother said. "Anna Rodriguez just paid me some money she owed me, so I'm sending it to you Western Union. You can pick it up at the office on University and Oak."

"How much?" I asked.

"Two hundred," she said. "Is that enough?"

"It'll do," I said. "Thank you."

Clothes, computer, college diploma, Book of Shadows. The landlord could sell the rest for back rent, or throw it out for all I cared. I loaded the car.

I piled the computer equipment on the desk and looked around. My mother had kept my bedroom the unchanged, which meant that the Backstreet Boys posters had to go.

I hung up my clothes in the closet, next to my prom dress and cap and gown, both wrapped in plastic. I pulled the thumbtacks out of the posters and rolled them up to store them in the closet. Then I flopped down onto the bed, still fully clothed, and slept.

When I woke up, I set up my computer. I'd have to ask Mom to get dial-up so I could email out resumes. I headed downstairs, where Mom waited at the table.

"Phew," she said, and wrinkled her nose.

"Can we get some kind of Internet so I can email out resumes?"

"Does that work?" She poured me a cup of coffee. "In my day, we pounded the pavement."

"Well," I said, "you didn't write websites."

She shrugged. "Maybe you should consider something else, since that's so slow. Substitute teaching. Clerical work."

I made a face. I'd tried that. They said that they wouldn't take me for either, since I was likely to leave them the second anything came along in my field. Ha. I'd been unemployed for two years, ever since the company went under, and no amount of magic seemed to get me a job.

"I'm sorry," she said, raising her hands. "I always end up saying the wrong thing. If your father were here..."

I sighed. "Is there anything I can do to help?"

"I have some software I'd like you to install," she said. "You know I'm hopeless. Your father always handled the computer. Quickbooks. Jennifer says that she couldn't run her shop without it, so I bought it and now I can't figure out how to set it up." She laughed. "Hopeless."

"I'd be happy to," I said.

"Just sign up for whatever you need; you can put it on my credit card." She stood and poured herself more coffee, then looked at me. "Have you tried prosperity spells?" she said.

No, Mother, that never occurred to me.

"I miss him, too," she said.

"Sometimes I think I would give up ten years of my life to get him back."

"Don't you say that," she said. She grabbed the salt shaker and rushed to the sink, filling a glass with water and pouring salt in. She sprinkled me with salt water, then picked up the knife from the butter dish and drew a circle on the kitchen floor around me. "You came from the ocean; the ocean will protect you," she said, and sprinkled me with more salt water. "Never say anything like that again."

My father's Book of Shadows had a spell to raise the dead. It was tucked in between the spell to meet your true love and the spell they used to conceive me, which partially involved making love on the beach—too much information, if you ask me. The spell was about a third of the way in, written in his youthful handwriting. Based on the surrounding spells, he'd probably learned it from Nana or maybe even great-Aunt Carmella.

In the margin, he had written, "Don't even think about it, Sandy," in the shaky, pain-addled scrawl he used at the end of his life. I was angry. Partly because I was tempted. I really would give ten years of my life to get him back, but I knew that wouldn't be enough. Besides, I knew my father wouldn't want me to shorten my life for his and that was the price. We're all born with a finite bit of life, and if I wanted him to have more, I had to give him some of mine.

At the bottom of the page in his normal handwriting, I read "Sandy, ocean child, my greatest bit of magic, my baby girl."

I couldn't see the page any more; my eyes were blurry with tears. I closed the book.

"Hail, Athena, Lady of Wisdom," I said, and lit a candle. "I'm here to ask for a job. It's been two long years, Lady, and since it was a very mental job, I'm asking You for Your help."

I put a resume in the candle flame. It wasn't much of an exchange, but it was the best I had. The resume wouldn't light, no matter how long I held the paper in the flame. I lowered the paper and extinguished the flame.

Offering rejected.

I was desperate and not yet ready to give up. So I relit the candle. "Hail, Athena, Lady of Wisdom. I need a job. Please help me."

I placed the resume in the candle flame. It still wouldn't light. I lowered the page, and the flame spread across the underside and singed my fingers. I dropped the resume and swore.

At which point it ignited, taking the carpet with it.

"Fuck!" I leapt to my feet and stomped on the flames until they were out. Then I extinguished the candle.

As omens went, this was bad.

I hit send on the last set of resumes and hung up the connection. That made twenty today.

I headed downstairs, and found my mother, who asked me to set the table for dinner.

I picked up two plates, two forks, and two knives and walked into the dining room. I put a plate, a fork, and a knife at each end of the table. I turned to go back into the kitchen, when something on the mantel caught my eye.

It was a large urn.

I stepped a little closer. Unmarked.

Mom came in with a bowl of mashed potatoes and a plate with corn on the cob.

"Is that...?" I asked.

"I forgot you hadn't seen that," she said. "Yes, it's your father."

My father. *My father.*

"You should have gone to the funeral," she said. "You would have found it comforting... Sandy?"

I realized I was shaking. Mom came over and put her arms around me, but I couldn't take my eyes off the mantel. It was like a part of me was trapped in that jar.

"Honey?"

"It's so small," I said. "It's just wrong that it would be so small." Intellectually, I knew that the human body was sixty percent water, but... no. Wrong.

"I'm sorry," she said. "I didn't realize you'd react like this. I would have taken it upstairs or something."

"We were just going to eat with him in that..."

"Would you rather eat in the kitchen?"

I shook my head and shuffled back to my chair.

Mom gave me a skeptical look and came back with a plateful of meatloaf.

Dead burnt flesh. Like my father, dead in a jar.

I waved the plate away, nauseated, and picked up an ear of corn.

"Are you sure?" she asked.

I nodded and spread butter on the corn.

She cut into her meatloaf with a knife. It was like watching someone cut Daddy. I couldn't watch her eat.

I burst into tears, clapped a hand over my mouth, and raced to the bathroom.

It was just wrong, and it had to change. He shouldn't have died. Not yet; it was too soon. He was too young. It was wrong. I could feel it in my gut.

I had the urn. The other things weren't difficult to get: sea water, a snakeskin, a robin's egg, some herbs. The sea water being my special protector was encouraging, although I knew I couldn't rely on that.

I didn't know how he would come back to me, if he would still be him. And there were practical things to consider: taxes, health insurance, the insurance money for his death—would we have to return the money? Would he still have cancer? Would we be taking him away from a better place?

I suppose this is why no one does this sort of spell. But I needed to make things right--and his counsel, and his faith--even if he would be angry with me.

"Hail, Hecate," I said, standing in a circle of seawater where three roads met. I laid the robin's egg and the snakeskin on the makeshift altar. "I offer part of my life for more time with my beloved father. Come back to me, Daddy."

Lightning flashed, and the wind rose, but there was no rain. The ceramic urn shook, then exploded.

I wasn't sure I wanted to look, but I couldn't help myself. Inside the shards was something that looked like a shriveled fetus. It grew, and was then a small, spindly boy with sad eyes. He had cuts on his arms from the shards.

"Sandy, no," he said.

I wanted to speak, but I felt a sudden, unbelievable pain in my legs. I fell to the ground and screamed, and he reached out and touched my arm. His hand was cold, so cold.

"You don't have enough life left in you to trade for mine," he said.

A large clump of my hair fell out, landing on my shoulder, then blowing away in the wind. "It's the chemo, isn't it?" I said.

He nodded. "I don't think either of us will last until dawn."

"Are you mad at me?" I asked.

"No," he said. "I should have known. Like father, like daughter."

It had never crossed his mind that I couldn't do it. Oh, Daddy. I've missed you.

"You were only four when the car hit you," he said. "I couldn't see the license plate, it was moving too fast. I looked down at my baby girl. You weren't moving, your legs crushed, your neck at an unnatural angle, blood coming out of your mouth. So I gathered you up in my arms and took you to a place where three roads met. Lucky we were vacationing at the beach, I guess. There were robins nesting in front of the cabin, and I remember thinking this must be why I'd found a snakeskin the other day. It was meant to be." He looked at me, his eyes curious. "You don't remember, do you?"

I shook my head. "I remember waking up in a place where three roads met. You told me I'd fallen down and hurt myself and asked if I felt better. Was that it?"

He nodded. "I should have told you. I thought you wouldn't want to know something fated you to die young. I'm sorry."

"And you got cancer," I said. "I'm so sorry."

"What parent wouldn't do the same, if he could?"

"I wish I'd told Mom where I was going," I said.

"She wouldn't approve."

"No."

"I didn't tell her, either," he said. "I always felt guilty about that." He looked down at the urn. "If she comes here, maybe she'll figure it out on her own."

"Great Aunt Carmella did it, too, didn't she?" I asked.

He smiled at me. "Smart girl. That's why she and my cousin Steve both died so young." He made a face. "Your mother thought it was dangerous and wrong. I suppose she was right."

"Poor Mom," I said, and felt tears prickle my eyes. I reached up and rubbed them away.

"Like father, like daughter," Daddy said, and patted my arm again.

"How have you been?" he asked.

"I hate having to move in with Mom. I hate the idea that she thinks I'm a loser."

"You could never disappoint us."

I snorted. "She's not your mother," I said.

"I think I know her better than you do." He laughed. "You're just like her sometimes."

I made a face.

The sun rose. Daddy was now some kind of shriveled baby-sized thing, dry and dusty, but he could speak. I reached out a hand, wrinkled and gnarled and swollen with arthritis, and brushed back the wispy remains of his hair. I told him about the coworker I'd had a crush on, about the cute guy who came into the occult bookstore I'd frequented back in Atlanta and bought crystals, about anything but regret because regret didn't matter. It was a fair exchange.

We were joined. Fated. It was meant to be.

As the sun rose, he crumbled into dust and I cried. My hands looked normal again, but they ached. The arthritis was probably permanent, and I suspected I had cancer—in my bone marrow, like Daddy had. It just made sense.

I couldn't gather up the ashes and take them with me, especially not with my hands so stiff. He was already being dispersed by the wind.

I could really use medical insurance right about now.

I tried to stand and couldn't; my hips and legs didn't seem to work right. So I lay back and watched the sunrise, and then my feet and legs stopped hurting.

I looked down, and they had crumbled into dust. My hands were disintegrating. I'd known the price was part of my life, I'd just thought I had more life to trade. I guess everyone does. But it was a fair trade; it was enough.

There wasn't anything to do about it, and I'd gotten what I wanted. So I stopped looking and watched the wind move the leaves overhead instead. And then I was the wind, and the leaves, and the Book of Shadows lying open on a large stone. And my father.

Love Stories

Grandfather Paradox

Ann stuffed her blood-spattered clothes into the next door apartment complex's dumpster. He wasn't dead, but it was harder to get a knife through someone's chest than she'd expected. Maybe he'd bleed to death before someone found him. She didn't care either way. She was a juvenile, so it wasn't like she was going to fry.

She walked. The YMCA was open. She locked herself in the men's room, curled up on the floor, and fell asleep.

The next morning, she stopped at an IHOP and told a grey-haired waitress, "I don't have any money, but can I have a cup of coffee?" The waitress must have felt sorry for her: she bought her breakfast. Afterwards, she went to Safeway and hid a steak and a bottle of beer under her coat and walked out. And kept walking. Someone had a barbecue grill in their back yard. She took it, and the charcoal, too.

What she could really go for now was some mushrooms. She should swipe some Kool-Aid and find a cow pasture. Or maybe she could rob a veterinary clinic. Anything to get the thought of him touching her out of her head, and that beer wasn't going to cut it.

Steak and beer. Almost luxurious.

The sign read "Open House." Yes, that sounded about perfect. She spent the night there on the carpet smelling faintly of shampoo.

It had happened to him, too. What her father had done to her, his father had done to him. Which, in her opinion, just made it worse. He knew what it was like.

When the police arrived and told her she was under arrest for murder, she couldn't stop laughing.

JANUARY 4, 2014

The crane lifted the sealed concrete container out of the hole in the ground. Ann lay down in the snow next to the hole and reached inside. "My arms are too short," she said.

Martin lay down next to her.

"Excuse me?" Dr. Chandler, the president of the university, said.

"I'm sorry," Martin said. "I thought my department chair had spoken to you. Martin Robbins, physics. My head programmer, Ann O'Connell. Please, continue."

Dr. Chandler gave them a dirty look, then walked over to the microphone. "This time capsule was sealed in 1914. The items inside represent what they wanted us to know about the past. I'm sure our history department is hoping I'll cut the speech short and let them get at it..."

There was a chuckle from the crowd.

"Got it," Martin said. He pulled out a grimy Tyvek envelope and opened it. Inside, there was a penny dated 2013. Martin smiled at her. "Looks like our own time capsule arrived intact."

FEBRUARY 9, 2014

"How are you feeling today, Ann?" Dr. Katz asked. Her glasses were perched precariously on her nose, and her bun was in danger of falling down.

Screw her. "Is my hour up yet?"

"No."

Fine. Be that way.

"How are things going with Martin?"

"I stopped dating Martin."

"Why?"

"Because he wanted to sleep with me. It was awful. Ugh."

Dr. Katz was giving Ann that psychiatrist look. Well, Ann had felt like she had to. Saying no would be rude. Well, not rude, but... Anyway, no more Martin. She'd had her phone number changed, and if he came around again? Restraining order. Work the system or the system works you.

"How does that affect your job?" Dr. Katz asked.

"I have vacation time," Ann said. "I took it."

Dr. Katz looked like she felt sorry for her. Ann hated that.

Dr. Katz asked, "Do you have any remorse over your father?"

"Do you think I should?" Ann asked.

"I was asking you," she said. Crafty. Ann guessed that was why she paid her the big bucks.

"Is my hour up yet?"

"I know you're tired of my asking you that, but you've never answered."

Ann shrugged and looked away.

"Do you really think his dying made your life any better?"

No. Ann didn't have to live with him any more, but it still happened.

Hmm. Maybe Dr. Katz was worth the money Ann paid her after all.

FEBRUARY 10, 2014

Martin looked skittish. Well, Ann supposed she didn't blame him.

"I'm sorry I... whatever it was I did," Martin said.

"It's not you," Ann said, and smiled the most charming smile she could muster. "It's me."

Martin just looked confused. Confused and skeptical.

"Can we take it slower?" Ann said.

"You tell me," Martin said.

Ann looked away. "How's the project?"

Oh, he seemed so excited she'd asked. "After the penny," he said, "we tried animal subjects, but it's a lot harder to confirm that those arrived safely. We think they did."

Perfect. "Will you show me the notes?"

Martin seemed to consider it. "Well," he said. "I suppose you do work here."

NOVEMBER 11, 1955

Ann dropped her blood-spattered lab coat in an alley and hotwired the car. It was an older model, of course—perhaps she should say "contemporary model" instead—but those were easier. Billy Watson had taught her how to hotwire cars in exchange for a blow job. She'd promptly stolen his car.

Grandfather was in the phone book. They lived out in the suburbs.

Time to change a little history.

DECEMBER 25, 1988

Ann sat on the floor with her Raggedy Ann doll. Her grandmother was in the kitchen, cooking. Daddy was... well, she wasn't sure where he was.

"Ann? Sweetie?"

Ann looked up.

Ann's grandmother was holding a sheet of cookies fresh out of the oven. "Where's your father?"

"Outside, I think."

"Go and tell him Christmas dinner is ready."

Ann put on her coat and gloves, and picked up her doll. She went outside, shutting the door behind her. "Daddy?" she said.

There was no answer, but there were footprints leading to the back yard, already filling up with snow. Daddy was lying in a snowdrift with a bottle, his eyes closed. He was covered in a light layer of snow, too, melting off his face, but clinging to his eyelashes.

"Daddy?"

He opened his eyes.

Ann didn't know what to say. She thought she should know. She was nine years old, not a baby any more. But she stood there, clutching her doll and looking at him.

He sighed, and sat up, and said, "What's up, baby girl?"

"Dinner is ready," Ann said.

Daddy started to cry. He dried his eyes and wiped his nose on his sleeve, then took Ann's hand and went into the house with her.

"You're drunk," Grandmother said. "Couldn't you just behave yourself for one day?"

"He put his cigarettes out on my arm," Daddy said. "Look!" He tried to roll up his sleeve and failed.

Grandmother started to cry. Ann stood there in her coat and hugged her doll.

AUGUST 12, 1989

The car came to a stop in front of their house. "Thank you for taking me, Mrs. King," Ann said.

"It was good having you with us," Mrs. King said. "It's a shame your father doesn't take you camping more often."

"He gets sick a lot," Ann said.

"I'll wait here and make sure you get inside okay."

Ann climbed out of the station wagon and retrieved her backpack. She walked up the sidewalk and unlocked the front door. She opened the door, and Mittens the cat rushed out. There was an awful smell.

Mittens cried, a mournful meow.

Ann stepped in, cautious, slow, walking towards...

She screamed, and ran out the door. Mrs. King was starting to drive away. She chased the station wagon, and Mrs. King stopped. She climbed in.

"Drive," Ann said.

"What's the matter, Ann?"

"Wait! I want Mittens!"

"Ann?"

"Wait!" Ann opened the car door and picked up the cat, then got back in and shut the door.

Mrs. King just looked at her.

"He's dead," Ann said, and started to cry.

FEBRUARY 9, 2014

"If I could give my father one gift," Ann told Dr. Katz, "I would give him a happy childhood."

She wasn't a detective, but she wanted to solve her grandfather's murder. She'd read all the newspaper accounts. If it wasn't for grandfather's murder, Daddy would still be alive.

"Maybe we should talk about the abortion," Dr. Katz said.

"I panicked," Ann said. "I just don't think I'm psychologically healthy enough to be a parent."

"And Martin?"

"We're getting a divorce."

"How does that affect your job?"

"It's a bit uncomfortable," Ann said. "But it's not like we aren't professionals."

Ann had been afraid for a moment that Martin would change the access codes, but that was silly. She was divorcing, not fired, and the wheels of academe turn slowly.

Maybe she could set things right once and for all. She wasn't sure what would happen to her, but maybe she could make things right for Daddy.

NOVEMBER 11, 1955

Ann sold her engagement ring and bought a car. Finding the house was easy; she'd lived there after Daddy died.

Grandmother was a tired-looking woman on the front porch with a black eye. "Don't remarry," Ann said.

"I beg your pardon?" Grandmother said.

Ann's timing must have been off, because the man who came to the front door wasn't her step-grandfather.

"Remarry?" he said. "Who are you?"

"A friend," Ann said.

"Eileen ain't got no friends," he said. "Get off my porch."

Grandmother looked scared, so she did. She headed down to the edge of the property.

That's where Ann saw her. Herself. Whoever. If this whole time-travel thing became common, the linguistics people were going to have a problem. She didn't know how this was possible, but she supposed time-travel was really Martin's area. Although she suspected he'd be unsettled to meet himself, too.

"Fancy meeting you here, doppelganger," the other Ann said. "Guess I didn't quite get this one right."

There were raised voices coming from the house. Grandmother screamed.

"If she loses the baby, we're both done for," Ann said.

"We can take him," the other Ann said. "The two of us? No problem."

"What?"

The other Ann gave her a scornful look. "You're not scared of him, are you? The things father did to us, he did to father first. He deserves to die." She beckoned. "Come on. We'll get it over with."

"You think I came here to kill him?"

"You didn't?" the other Ann said. "Why did you come?"

NOVEMBER 11, 1955

Ann hated her doppelganger.

Ann shouldn't hate her doppelganger. She made her. She was her: the Ann she wanted to be, the Ann she created by coming back to kill Grandfather. She thought she'd love her, but no, seeing her, she was so full of hate and envy her throat was full and she couldn't breathe.

If she was going to kill for her, shouldn't she love her?

"Apparently," her doppelganger said, sitting on the ground, "Grandmother has no taste. Her next husband was a bastard, too."

Damn. Ann had never thought of that. "Well," she said, "we can't have a long line of us coming back in time to kill her husbands, can we?"

Doppelganger Ann laughed a little. "No. Maybe if we called Child Protective Services..."

"I don't think they have Child Protective Services yet."

"The police?"

"For an unborn child?" Which meant that they couldn't just cut to the chase and kill Grandmother, unfortunately.

"What are we going to do, then?"

"I can't not kill Grandfather," Ann said, sitting on the ground next to her. "You'll cease to exist if I don't."

"I don't want you to kill anyone," the doppelganger said.

"We're all born of original sin," Ann said. "Except you. You were born of my sin."

Somehow Ann didn't think that was what her doppelganger wanted to hear. "There's more than just cause and effect going on here," the doppelganger said.

"Ethos anthropos daimon. Character is fate. Maybe if we changed Grandmother somehow."

Apparently, they'd taken similar coursework in college. "Character is created by cause and effect," Ann said.

The doppelganger shook her head. "No. I have no control over the things that happened to me, but I can control how I react to them. That's character."

"You may have free will," Ann said, "but not me. I am a product of causal determinism."

"Don't be such a fatalist."

"You know," Ann said, "we can argue free will all day, but right now, I have a child molester to kill. What say we continue this philosophical discussion later, over wine and cheese?"

"But this impacts whether what you do makes any difference!"

"Either way," Ann said, "I'm performing a service to society and I suggest you not interfere."

"But he hasn't done anything yet!"

"How do you know?" Ann stood.

Her doppelganger stood, too. "I can't let you do this."

"I'll say it again: stay out of my way."

At least her doppelganger seemed to have the wit to be scared. She stood aside, and Ann went back into the house. Grandmother was weeping at the foot of the stairs. Grandmother started when she saw her, but Ann put a finger over her lips and mouthed, "Gun."

Grandmother looked at Ann like she was her savior, and pointed at the back door. There was a shotgun next to it. Ann picked it up and started up the stairs, moving as quietly as she could.

He was lying on the bed, looking at the ceiling. He saw her peering around the corner. "What the hell do you want?" he asked. "How did you...?"

She pointed the shotgun at him. "I know what you are. I know what you're going to do to Eileen's child."

He sat up and stared, looking terrified.

"It happened to you, too, didn't it?"

"I don't know what you're talking about."

"Wrong answer," she said, and pulled the trigger. It went straight through his heart, which was probably an easier death than he deserved, but in a sense he was a victim, too. What happened to her happened to him. But what happened to her happened because of him, because of what he did, because of what happened to him.

Stop the cycle. I want to get off.

NOVEMBER 11, 1955

Grandmother looked at her so strangely when she came in the front door, but otherwise she took a second Ann surprisingly well. "I'm not her,? Ann said.

Grandmother looked up the stairs, then raised an eyebrow at Ann.

She probably only had a moment. "Listen to me," Ann said. "No matter how nice he seems, don't marry the investigating officer."

"How will I support my child if I don't remarry?"

"Can you move back in with your parents?"

"I wouldn't raise a child in my father's house," she said.

Oh.

There was a gunshot upstairs.

"Don't touch the gun," Ann said. "It'll have her fingerprints on it. Say it was a strange woman, say you think your husband was having an affair with her, they'll believe you." After all, it worked the first time.

"Who are you?" she said.

"We're your granddaughter," Ann said. Grandmother seemed to take that better than Ann expected.

The other Ann came barreling down the stairs. "Time to go, doppelganger." She looked at Grandmother. "Don't touch the gun. Call the police."

Grandmother nodded.

"Don't forget what I told you to tell them," Ann said. "They'll never believe the truth."

"I don't think I believe the truth," she said.

NOVEMBER 11, 1955

They ducked under a bridge. "Well, this sucks," the other Ann said.

"What?"

"I was hoping that I would cease to exist at this point," she said. "I guess it doesn't work that way."

Ann heard a car come to a stop on the bridge over them, and ducked under a bush into the mud. She heard the other Ann make a disgusted noise, and the car doors opened, followed by the sound of footsteps.

"Come out with your hands up," a voice said. "This is the police. You're under arrest for the murder of Charles O'Connell."

The other Ann started to laugh.

JANUARY 19, 1956

Grandmother brought a date to the trial, a good-looking older guy who appeared to have money. Ann didn't like the way he kept his hand on her back. Possessive. Like he owned her. On the other hand, there were only two Anns running around so far, which might be a good sign.

The other Ann pled guilty and suggested the death penalty. The judge looked disturbed by that and sentenced her to life in prison.

Ann found herself thinking of Martin. She supposed that it didn't matter what she did now. Unless, of course, she wanted to steal her father from her grandmother and raise him herself. She still didn't think she'd make a great parent, although she figured she couldn't do that much worse than grandmother. But she'd had her chance and she'd aborted it. So she bought herself a big bottle of vodka, and found herself a nice snowdrift to drink it in.

JANUARY 4, 2014

The crane lifted the sealed concrete container out of the hole in the ground. Martin lay down in the snow next to the hole and reached inside. Ann stood next to him, her hand resting on her pregnant belly.

Martin pulled out a grimy Tyvek envelope. "Got it!" he said.

Ann threw her arms around his neck and kissed him.

Love Stories

In Sickness and in Health

Robbie didn't sleep, but if he did, the the sound of Lydia vomiting would have woken him up. It echoed all up and down the house through the plumbing.

He padded downstairs, watching his feet. They looked indistinguishable from human feet, if perhaps less veiny. He went into the guest bedroom downstairs where Lydia had moved because her bones were getting brittle, and moved into the bathroom.

Lydia was clinging to the toilet, which had a height adjuster on it because she sometimes had trouble getting up after using it. She was pale and her knuckles were even paler from the effort of clinging to the height adjuster. Robbie leaned over and pulled her red hair back, then reached over and picked up a band to tie it back with. Some of it came out in his hands. He slipped it into a wastebasket behind Lydia's back.

"I'm sorry," Lydia said.

"Don't be," Robbie said, and he meant it. He might malfunction again someday, too. Lydia had had to replace his spine after he'd damaged it moving her into her new house. Most people would have just replaced him, but Lydia said she was fond of him. She'd had to sign a waiver saying he hadn't been engaged in paid labor at the time of damage, too. Apparently, some people thought they could get around the android labor laws by operating on a cash-only basis. They weren't the sort to fix a broken unit, though.

"I think I'm finished," Lydia said, her voice thick. She spat into the toilet.

Robbie flushed, then helped her up. He kept one arm around her as he poured her a cup of water to rinse out her mouth.

"I don't know what I'd do without you," Lydia said. She took a big sip of water, swished it around, and spat. What she spat out was discolored. She scowled at the mirror and sighed. "There's no way in hell I can go to work today. I can barely stand up by myself."

"I can make you some breakfast," Robbie said.

Lydia made a face. "Nothing tastes good except popsicles. If you want to bring me one..."

Robbie helped Lydia to the bed and then popped off to the kitchen. He got a popsicle out of the freezer, unwrapped it, wrapped the stick handle in a paper towel in case it melted, and returned to the guest bedroom.

Lydia was sitting propped up in the corner of the bed. It was a hospital bed, with railings, and she'd piled up a bunch of pillows to support her back. Robbie sat on the bed as lightly as he could and handed her the popsicle.

"Thank you, sweetheart," Lydia said. She put the popsicle in her mouth and made a loud slurping noise. "Sorry."

"I don't mind," Robbie said.

Lydia smiled at him. "Sit closer."

Robbie edged closer to Lydia and she put her head on his shoulder and nibbled the popsicle. Robbie felt a deep sense of satisfaction. This was what he was made for: being useful. He just hated the circumstances.

Lydia finished her popsicle and handed Robbie the stick. He laid it on the nightstand, careful not to let any popsicle juice drip on it.

"I think I need to sleep," Lydia said.

Robbie picked her up like she was a small child and tucked her in. He gathered up the popsicle remains, drew her blinds, and turned out the light. "Sleep well."

Lydia's voice was tired but had a spark of her old humor to it. "I'll do my best."

Robbie closed the door. He went into the kitchen and tidied things up: sweeping, mopping, taking out the trash. There weren't any dishes to do. He didn't want to run the vacuum while Lydia was sleeping, so he dusted instead.

The phone rang. Robbie tried to answer it before it woke Lydia, but he was too late. He picked up the extension to hear Lydia say, "Oh, shit. I'm sorry. I forgot to call in."

There was cold silence on the other end of the line.

"I couldn't sleep last night because I was up all night vomiting. I'm so sorry."

"You're out of sick time," the man on the other end of the phone said.

"I know," Lydia said, "but as you may recall, I have cancer. Just dock my pay like you did last time."

"No, Lydia," the man said, "I think it's time that you faced facts. You're disabled. You can't work. Either you go on disability or I fire you."

Lydia hung up on him. Robbie hung up, too, and went into Lydia's bedroom.

"They're a fucking hospital!" Lydia said. "I have fucking cancer!"

Robbie did a quick web search through his built-in network connection. "It's financially better for you if you go on disability. You'll make less money, but your medical bills are more likely to be covered."

Lydia burst into tears, and Robbie sat next to her and held her. He wiped her eyes and nose with his sleeve, which made her laugh. Then she picked up the phone and dialed.

"So, Chris," she said. "If I go on disability, I keep my health benefits, right?"

There was a pause.

"I have long-term and short-term disability. Yeah. Well, you're going to have to fax or courier the paperwork over because I can't come in. Okay, bye." She hung up the phone and then said, "Fuck you, Chris."

Robbie didn't know what to say to that.

"I need to go back to sleep," Lydia said, and unplugged the phone. "We're now making half of what I made before, but since I can't eat anything except popsicles and you don't eat, we should be able to keep the house. Thank God I never got a dog."

Robbie stood and walked over to the door and turned out the light.

The phone rang. Robbie picked it up before the ringing could disturb Lydia. "Hello?"

The voice on the other end was an unfamiliar man. "Hello, may I speak to Lydia Anderson?"

"She's resting. Can I help you?"

"Just tell her her cousin Bob called," the man said. "Let me give you a number so she can call me back."

"Lydia doesn't have a cousin Bob," Robbie said.

"Am I speaking to Mr. Anderson?"

Robbie didn't have a last name, being manufactured and all, but he supposed that Lydia's last name was fine for him. "Yes."

"Mr. Anderson, I'm calling about your wife's outstanding balance at Lakeview Memorial Hospital. Are you aware that her outstanding balance is $113,521.43 and that she has failed to make her minimum payment of $2,561 for the past three months?"

His wife. Well, Lydia was as close to a wife as he was likely to have, so he answered, "Are you aware that my wife has breast cancer?"

"Federal privacy regulations prohibit the hospital from sharing that information with us, sir. The only information we're provided is the outstanding balance."

"My wife is dying," Robbie said, and the amount of emotion that went into saying that surprised him. "Leave her alone."

"I'm sorry to hear that, sir," the man said, "but she's

still alive and has incurred financial obligations. Obligations that you, as her husband, share."

Robbie was sure that he could tell the man that he was an android and get him to shut up. Androids didn't have financial responsibilities. They couldn't hold jobs, or have bank accounts in their names, or own property. Androids were property. People who charged other people for their android's labor were fined and their androids were confiscated. Androids who decided to break the labor laws on their own were wiped.

It occurred to Robbie that if he told the man he was an android, he might be seized and sold to pay Lydia's debts, so he hung up on him.

He wondered what would happen if they seized the house. Where Lydia would live. She didn't have any family except him, and he didn't count.

He might not be Lydia's husband, but he shared her obligations. She'd taken care of him for years and now he wanted to return the favor.

Robbie applied for several jobs online claiming to be Robert Anderson, Lydia's husband. Despite knowing about the android labor laws, he had no idea how one got an illegal job. So instead, he applied for things like tech support: things that had searchable solutions but didn't require excessive documentation.

People kept calling for Lydia. He would refuse to put them through, even though their excuses for why they should be allowed to talk to her became more and more extreme. He just told them he was Lydia's husband and they could tell him anything they wanted to tell her. Usually, all they wanted to tell her was that she owed the hospital money. Robbie already knew that and didn't need to be told repeatedly.

Finally, someone called asking for him. He was wary, but it turned out to be a local software company looking for tech support. One of the jobs he'd applied for! He set up an interview but didn't tell Lydia. She slept most of the time, anyway, except when she needed to go to the doctor or was throwing up.

He felt guilty when he went shopping for job interview clothes, but he figured it would turn out all right if he got the job.

The interview was fast. They asked him a bunch of questions about computers. He had a built-in Internet connection in his head so he could find the answers online. They told him they were impressed with his knowledge and asked him to start work on Monday.

They also asked him for documentation—a driver's license, a marriage license. He ended up driving down to the crappy part of town looking for shady characters who might get him to a good forger. He asked people in bars and hanging around on street corners. Finally, a man said, "I know someone. How do I know you're not a cop?"

"I'm an android," Robbie said. "Androids aren't allowed to be cops."

They stared at each other for a moment, and then the man got into the car. He directed Robbie until they got to a house. It was probably the nicest house in the neighborhood, but that wasn't saying a lot.

"Don't judge," the man said. "I send most of the money home to my wife."

He got out of the car. Robbie followed. The inside of the house had a sectional sofa and a big screen television, but no other amenities. He led Robbie into a back bedroom and took his picture, then led him back into the living room.

"That'll be eight hundred bucks," the man said.

Lydia didn't have eight hundred dollars in her checking account, the only account to which Robbie had access. "That might present a problem."

"What about your car?" the man asked.

Robbie thought about it. He and Lydia had separate cars from when she worked. She didn't really need a car any more. She couldn't drive because she couldn't turn her head and had a tendency to vomit unexpectedly. On the other hand, the car was worth more like a thousand. "Throw in a marriage license and you have a deal."

The man shook his hand and Robbie handed him the car keys. The man told Robbie to watch television.

About an hour later, the man handed Robbie his driver's license. Robbie had better-than-average vision but didn't see any signs of forgery on it.

"I have the same equipment the DMV uses," the man said. "It's best if you don't ask where I got it."

Robbie wasn't really that curious. He put the driver's license in his wallet.

Then the man handed him his marriage license. It was pretty, with delicate little flowers and wedding bells inscribed on it, and his and Lydia's names. If he were human, he would have cried. When he looked up, the man was watching him, looking curious.

"I'm doing this for her," Robbie said.

The man drove Robbie back to Lydia's house and Robbie got the car title to sign over to the man.

"Aren't you going to ask my name?" the man asked.

"Should I?"

The man laughed. "Probably not, but most people do."

Robbie just smiled and handed the man the car title.

"Good luck with your lady friend," the man said.

There wasn't any luck to be had. Lydia would die. But Robbie smiled and thanked the man, anyway.

When he got back, Lydia hadn't even realized he had gone. As near as he could tell, she'd slept the whole time, and she didn't wake up when he came into her room. She looked restful, peaceful, but her eyes were a little sunken. He pocketed her car keys and wondered if he should make dinner.

He waited to see if Lydia could eat dinner and lay down on the couch. He did searches of information that might be useful to a tech support job.

Lydia didn't wake until 3 in the morning. She was ravenous, but nothing tasted good. "It all tastes metallic," she said, forcing down Robbie's hamburger. "I'm sure it's delicious," she said, her voice apologetic.

"It's all right," Robbie said. They sat on the couch together and channel-surfed. Lydia fell asleep with her head on his shoulder.

He picked her up and carried her back to bed. She'd lost three pounds this week, and she didn't really have it to lose. He wondered what he could make for her that would taste good. He couldn't exactly feed her an entire box of popsicles. He tucked her in, and she slept through it.

The next morning at 6, he got up, dressed, and went to work. The car radio was still set to Lydia's classical music station. He left it. Lydia used to do this every morning. She used to stop at Starbucks and get coffee, though.

He didn't need to drink coffee.

He walked through the door and down the hall to Human Resources, like they'd told him to. They showed him a video about proper work behavior and a presentation about his health insurance. Then he filled out forms.

Dependents: one. Lydia Anderson, wife. He showed them his driver's license and marriage license.

The cube they led him to was small and noisy. He suspected the chair wasn't comfortable, although he didn't care about comfort. A man sat with him in the cube to train him, but when the first call came in, he did well enough that they left him alone.

When he got home, he could hear Lydia throwing up. He went into the bathroom and held her hair. Then he helped her stand.

"Do you want a popsicle?"

Lydia shuddered and made a face.

"Are you finished?"

Lydia winced and clutched her stomach. "I don't think there's anything left in there, but that's not a guarantee."

Robbie carried Lydia back to bed and tucked her in.

"Stay," she said.

So he curled up next to her and held her. She shivered and moved closer, and he turned up his internal thermostat so he would generate more heat.

"That's nice," she murmured, and then her breathing because regular. Robbie was afraid to move for fear that he might wake her. She was light and cold, and there were dark bags under her eyes.

Robbie's coworker, an overweight grey haired woman, stuck her head into his cube. "Hi. I'm Margot."

"Robbie."

"You're not going to work through lunch again, are you?" She smiled. "You're making the rest of us look bad."

"Oh," Robbie said, and stood. "I'm sorry."

"I was only teasing, bless your heart," Margot said.

"Oh," Robbie said, and sat back down. He could tell from Margot's expression that this was the wrong reaction. "I... perhaps I should go investigate the break room."

Margot nodded.

The two of them walked down the hall. There were people talking and laughing. Robbie poured himself a cup of coffee, even though he didn't need to eat.

"You didn't bring your lunch?"

"I forgot," Robbie said. "My wife is sick. I was up all night with her."

"I'm sorry," Margot said, and she sounded like she meant it. "What is it, the flu?"

"Breast cancer." He took a sip of coffee. The room became quiet. He looked around. "Was I not supposed to say that?"

"Will she live?" a young, skinny guy in the corner asked. The guy sitting next to him punched him in the arm. He winced. "Sorry!"

Robbie suspected that he shouldn't answer that question, so he put down his coffee and left. He stepped onto the back loading dock where people were smoking. Margot followed him.

"Pay no attention to Roger," she said. "He has no tact at all."

"I'm not offended," Robbie said.

"Well, that's very kind of you," Margot said. "Let me know if you need to talk, okay?"

"All right," Robbie said.

Margot went back into the building, and Robbie sat down on the stairs. He didn't really understand why he shouldn't answer when people asked him a question. If it didn't bother him to say that Lydia would die, why should it bother people to hear it?

After a while, he went back into the building and answered another call.

Lydia slept until he had to leave for work. She gave him a curious look.

"I need cleaning supplies," Robbie said.

Lydia nodded and got a glass of water, and Robbie left.

When he was at work, Robbie noticed that people were looking at him oddly and avoiding him. He didn't know what to do about it, so he ignored them.

Finally, around lunchtime, the skinny guy—Roger—came to Robbie's cube. "You're an Aspie, too, aren't you?"

"Aspie?" Robbie did a quick internet search. Asperger's Syndrome. An autism spectrum disorder characterized by difficulties in social interaction.

"Me, too," Roger said, and smiled. He tilted his head towards the cube opening. "They're so stupid. They think you're an android or something."

Oh, shit. "No, I just have Asperger's, like you said."

"I knew it!" Roger said. "Is your wife an Aspie, too?"

"No," Robbie said. "She was a nurse."

"Cool," Roger said. "Anyway, maybe bring in your paperwork before they ask you questions." He rolled his eyes. "It's so stupid."

"Yeah," Robbie said. "Thank you."

"You're welcome," Roger said. There was an awkward silence, and then he asked, "Is your wife going to die?"

"Yes," Robbie said.

"Are you okay?" Roger asked.

No one but Lydia had ever asked him that. He imagined that he'd cry if he were human. He could probably simulate it, but he doubted he'd be convincing. "I have to be okay," Robbie said. "There aren't any other options."

"Yeah," Roger said. "Take care of yourself."

"You, too," Robbie said. "And thank you again."

"The mutant brotherhood has to stick together," Roger said, and bumped fists with Robbie.

Robbie knocked on the door of the man who made his driver's license and marriage license. A woman answered the door. She turned and said something in a language Robbie didn't know, and then the man appeared.

"You need something else?" the man asked.

"A doctor's note saying that I have Asperger's Syndrome," Robbie said.

"Not so much with the social skills, eh?" the man said. "No problem, I can do that for you. What have you got to pay with?"

Robbie handed the man Lydia's mother's wedding ring.

The man took the ring, looked at it and shrugged, then went inside.

Robbie sat down on the porch and watched a bunch of children playing soccer in the street. He wondered what it was like to be a child. Or a parent, for that matter. He'd never be either. He wondered if he was missing out. Maybe he should ask Lydia what it was like to be a child when he got home. He shouldn't ask her about being a parent. She cried after her mastectomy because it meant she could never breastfeed a child.

The man came out with a piece of paper. It said that Robert Anderson had Asperger's Syndrome and had undergone social skills training.

"Thank you," Robbie said.

The man smiled at him. "How's your lady friend?"

"Very sick," Robbie said, but remembered not to add details. He might need more documents.

The man tilted his head at him, like he didn't want to ask.

"That's why I'm working," Robbie said. "I'm doing it for her."

The man nodded, then patted Robbie on the back and went back inside. He looked like he understood.

When he got home, Lydia was in the kitchen looking into the freezer. "I had no idea there were so many varieties of popsicles." Finally, she grabbed one that was banana-flavored and went to go sit on the couch with it.

"What was it like to be a child?" Robbie asked.

Lydia tilted her head at him. Finally, she said, "What a question! I don't know if I can explain it to you."

Robbie sat down next to her.

"Days were longer then. There was boredom, and feeling constrained. There was joy in play that lasted for hours and hours. And it was safe." Lydia slurped at her popsicle. "I ate a lot of these then, too."

Robbie smiled and leaned closer to her.

"It's strange to think about the beginning of life now that I'm at the end," Lydia said.

"Do you believe in an afterlife?" Robbie asked.

"No," she said. "You die, and they put you in the earth and you rot. The end." She sighed and slurped on her popsicle. "How about you?"

"If any of my data survives critical malfunction, it's unlikely that anyone will have any use for it," Robbie said. "Unless an owner requests otherwise, they will destroy my storage to protect your privacy."

"And then you go into the earth—the landfill, at any rate—and rust," Lydia said.

Robbie nodded. He found the idea unsettling on one hand, but oddly comforting on the other—to think Lydia and he would have the same lack of afterlife.

Lydia took his hand. "It's not so bad. I've had a good life. I had a job I loved helping people."

"So did I," Robbie said. He meant helping Lydia, not technical support.

Lydia kissed him on the cheek. "I should go to bed."

When Robbie came home from work the next day, Lydia was asleep. He cleaned and fussed and lay down on the couch. He checked on her on his way out the door. She was still asleep.

When he came home the night after that, she was still asleep. She was thin. Her skin was thin and dry, and when he pinched her arm her skin stayed tented up.

Lydia was dehydrated.

He spoke to her quietly, growing increasingly louder when she didn't respond. He shook her. He leaned down and listened to her breath for a moment, and then he picked her up in his arms and carried her out to the car.

He buckled her into the passenger seat; the belt holding her mostly upright. He started the car and drove. When she didn't react to the motion, he drove faster and ran a couple of red lights. A police car pulled behind him with its lights on. When Robbie didn't pull over, it pulled into the lane beside him.

Robbie rolled down his window and shouted, "Hospital!"

The officer nodded and pulled in front of him, lights still on. He followed the police car all the way to Lakeview Memorial Hospital, where Lydia used to work.

He picked her up and carried her into the Emergency Room.

"Oh, no," the nurse said. She called for a gurney and Robbie put Lydia down on it. "Lydia, can you hear me?"

There was no response, so they wheeled Lydia away.

The police officer stepped a little closer. "What happened?"

"She has cancer," Robbie said.

"I'm sorry," the officer said. "Can I see your driver's license?"

Robbie almost pulled out the fake driver's license, but remembered to give the officer his android license instead. Then he went to go talk to the other nurse. "What do you think will happen to her?"

"I'm sorry," she said. "I'm not allowed to offer prognoses." She looked away, at the floor, which Robbie assumed meant that Lydia would die.

The doctor came out and walked over to Robbie. "Are you an immediate family member?"

Robbie nodded.

"Well, it's not really an emergency because there's nothing we can do. We can check her in if you'd like, but she's not in any pain and she won't get better."

Robbie wondered if Lydia would rather die at home. Then he decided that if she didn't know where she was—and he was fairly certain she didn't—she should be where the doctors were. "I think she should stay." The doctor didn't answer, so he added, "She loved it here."

The doctor patted him on the shoulder and left.

The police officer came back and handed Robbie his driver's license. "Does she have any next of kin?"

Robbie shook his head.

"Are you a home health care model?"

"She originally purchased me for housekeeping with the possibility of childcare later, but downloaded a new instruction set when she got sick."

"Good," the officer said. "Keep up the good work." The officer left and Robbie sat down in the waiting room.

It occurred to him he should call in sick to work. He left a voicemail on his supervisor's phone saying that his wife was in the hospital and he wouldn't be in and sat back down.

The last people Robbie expected to see in the hospital waiting room were Margot and Roger. Margot had a foil-covered casserole dish, and Roger looked earnest and uncomfortable and carried a box of supermarket chocolate chip cookies.

"Are you okay?" Margot asked.

Robbie didn't know how to answer that, so he shrugged. Margot patted him, and Roger sat down next to him. There was an awkward silence, and then Margot peeled back the foil to expose homemade macaroni and cheese. Roger handed him the box of cookies.

"I'm not hungry," Robbie said.

"Of course you're not," Margot said, "but you should eat, anyway. When's the last time you ate?"

"I don't know," Robbie said.

"Exactly," Margot said and handed him a plastic fork.

Robbie didn't want to be rude, so he ate a little macaroni and cheese. He analyzed the taste. This was probably a traditional recipe. If Lydia had lived, he could have tried to reproduce it for her. "It's very good."

"Thank you," Margot said.

Robbie ate a serving of macaroni and one of Roger's cookies, and Margot and Roger stayed for about three hours. They didn't pester him, but Margot asked if he needed to go home and sleep. Robbie said no.

The doctor came out and walked over to Robbie. "I'm sorry, but Lydia is dead. You should go home now and await further instructions from the state."

"Can I see her?" Robbie asked.

The doctor raised an eyebrow, but he let Robbie come into the room. Lydia was pale, still. So thin. He touched her shoulder. Cold.

"It's a good thing she left instructions," the doctor said. "She had a living will on file. You don't have to do anything."

"What will happen to me?" Robbie asked.

"You'll be sold to help pay her debts," the doctor said. "It's all right. You should go home and await further instructions."

He'd be wiped to protect Lydia's privacy.

"All right," Robbie said, even though it wasn't all right. He didn't want to forget Lydia.

He went home and looked around. The only thing in the house that meant anything to him was Lydia's photo album. So he took it, and his clothes, and his first paycheck, and got in the car to head to Mexico. He could get a job there as Robert Anderson and live as a widower.

He cashed his paycheck and headed south, towards freedom.

Love Stories

In the Water

Yvonne looked up from her monitor, the beads in her cornrows clattering as Roger walked into her office.

Roger sat in the dark wooden chair opposite her desk. "Weren't you assigned Alice van Buuren?"

"Oh, no you don't," Yvonne said. "You can't have her." Yvonne hadn't been assigned Alice; she'd requested her. Alice was probably the only murder victim's wife she would ever meet. They hadn't even put the murder in the papers. Maybe they thought there'd be a panic.

"Please," Roger said. "I'm just trying to save you some trouble. I've already spoken to her, and..."

Yvonne crossed her arms and glared. "Wouldn't you raise hell if I talked to one of your patients behind your back?"

"She's refusing modern therapy. What are you going to do, use the old-fashioned techniques your grandmother used?"

Roger had a lot of nerve mentioning Grandma. Yvonne glanced at the photo on the corner of her desk. Grandma Jackson had been a big woman with braids down to her hips and skin like chocolate. Grandma Jackson smiled back at the camera, all reassuring good nature.

Roger said, "I think we should just wipe her and have done with it."

"Too bad she's not your patient," Yvonne said.

"I could take her away from you, you know."

"Don't you dare!"

There was an awkward silence.

"It'll be less confusing for her if I come with you," Roger said. "Just to hand her off to you. You understand."

"Fine," Yvonne said. "Whatever."

"Good girl," Roger said, and Yvonne gritted her teeth. "Room 314." He stood. "Let's go."

"Now?" Yvonne said. She picked up her coffee and almost took a sip, then put it down again, making a face. It was cold, and it had been so bitter hot that she'd taken caffeine pills with orange juice instead.

Roger snorted. "That bad?"

Roger clearly wasn't going anywhere, so Yvonne stood, picked up her jacket, and followed Roger out of her office. The halls were white to the point of being blinding after her calm, earth-toned office, and reeked of disinfectant.

They went upstairs and over to room 314. Roger placed his hand on the identification plate and the door slid open.

"Hello, Alice," Roger said.

The patient, a skinny, pale woman with brown hair, backed away from Roger. She reminded Yvonne of someone, although she couldn't put her finger on whom.

The patient fell into a seated position on the bed, mouth open, staring at Yvonne. Before Yvonne could say anything, Roger said, "This is Doctor Jackson. Doctor Jackson, this is Alice."

"We're not going to hurt you," Yvonne said.

The patient—Alice—stared at Yvonne for a moment, then shut her mouth. She shot Roger a defiant look.

"I'll just leave you to it," Roger said, and left.

"Hello, Alice," Yvonne said. "You can call me Yvonne if you prefer."

"We've met," Alice said. It wasn't a question.

Alice really did look familiar. "Refresh my memory?"

"It doesn't matter," Alice said and looked away.

There was an uncomfortable silence.

Yvonne said, "Doctor Hill said you're refusing drug therapy."

"I had a negative reaction once," Alice said.

"Really?" Yvonne said. "Usually that's associated with an interaction with an unapproved drug. You should be fine this time; your blood tests came back clean."

"I wasn't on anything then, either," Alice said.

"That's very unusual," Yvonne said.

Alice shrugged. "Just weird, I guess."

"He also said you object to memory modification."

Alice started to cry.

For a moment Yvonne just wanted to hug Alice and let her cry, but negative emotions caused crime. It wasn't right to encourage Alice to carry on. "You won't forget your marriage. We'll just erase the trauma of his murder. We can come up with a cover story for why he's gone together—a heart attack, perhaps—and then give you some antidepressants and send you on your way."

"I'm sorry," Alice said, and dried her eyes, sniffling. "It just feels like forgetting so soon would be wrong. I don't want to forget. I loved him."

"You won't forget. You just won't be upset."

"Which feels wrong."

"Well," Yvonne said, "you're not a danger to yourself or others, so I won't make you do anything you don't want to do. But we are going to keep you for observation."

"All right," Alice said.

Yvonne patted Alice on the shoulder. It seemed to make Alice nervous, so she decided not to do that again. "Get a good night's sleep. Let me know if you need something to help you rest."

"I'm fine," Alice said, although she didn't look fine at all.

Yvonne left and locked the door behind her, then clocked out and walked to the train station. The art display on the street corner was a holographic image of large fish swimming in a tank, which she always felt was very soothing and very appropriate to a hospital. Across the street, there was an escalator down to MARTA II, the commuter train.

The sun was setting, and the streetlights all up and down the street lit up in random pastel colors. The crosswalk signal chimed, and she crossed the street and took the escalator down to the commuter train, where most people were reading or sitting quietly. Some of them looked up and smiled; she smiled back. The station was decorated with statuary from the old days of Atlanta, some of the few architectural pieces that survived the civil war. Life had been so violent then, back before modern psychiatry.

The train arrived, and she found a seat and pulled out her latest issue of *Psychopharmacology Journal*. She'd barely finished the first article when she realized she was almost at her stop, so she put the journal away and looked around. Out the window, they were passing an old graveyard with Victorian monuments of stone angels. Yvonne liked to jog there in the mornings; Grandma Jackson was buried there.

The train pulled to a stop, and Yvonne got off and walked the four blocks to her house. It was dark now, but the city provided excellent lighting. She unlocked the door, went inside, and locked the door again. Locks on doors were really a throwback to her mother's time. One of these days she was going to decide it was just too silly and stop locking her door. Grandma always had a big key ring that Yvonne had played with as a child; Yvonne remembered the jangly noise and the metallic taste from chewing on them.

The computer and video were new, of course, but a lot of the furniture was old—her grandmother's. There was a Persian rug, the kind you couldn't get any more, and a grandfather clock, and books. Roger had told her to throw it all out. He said it was morbid, that it was holding her back, that she needed more therapy to get over Grandma's death. Asshole. She couldn't wait for him to retire.

On the contrary, she thought her house was just about perfect. The only thing missing was another person. Yvonne was so busy that it didn't leave much time for a social life. She couldn't remember the last time she'd had friends over. The truth was that she was lonely, and she couldn't even figure out why she wasn't doing anything about it.

She went into the kitchen and poured herself a glass of water. There was something in the smell she didn't like—something chemical—so she poured it out and got herself some milk instead.

Yvonne pulled one of Grandma's old psychology texts off the bookshelf. She put on her nightgown and went to read in bed. After a couple of hours, she took a Somnalix with a glass of warm milk and turned off the light.

She dreamed she and Alice were running away from some kind of monster—something out of the cheesy old horror movies her mother used to watch. She woke up in a cold sweat and swallowed a Valium dry, then went back to bed.

"You want to talk about it?" Yvonne asked Alice.

Alice shook her head. Her hair looked very dark against the stark white of the room and her hospital gown.

"Will you at least tell me how you're feeling this morning?"

Alice sighed. "I'm all right, how are you?"

"I'm good. I had a nice run this morning," Yvonne said. "You ever run?"

Alice shook her head. "I don't have the skin for outdoor exercise. I've already had one growth removed."

"I can get you some gym time, if you'd like," Yvonne said.

Alice snorted.

"Exercise is therapeutic," Yvonne said. "No one would object to my arranging something therapeutic for a patient."

"Thank you," Alice said. "I'd like that."

"You know," Yvonne said, "if you're not willing to take pharmacological treatment, you really should talk."

"You wouldn't believe me," Alice said.

"Try me."

Alice looked at her, and Yvonne suspected she was considering whether she wanted to talk or not. "What made you decide to become a psychiatrist?"

"My grandmother," Yvonne said, and smiled. "She was a psychiatrist, too. She helped a lot of people. When I was little, I wanted to be just like her."

Alice smiled. "Where is she now?"

"Dead," Yvonne said. "Heart attack."

They looked at each other for a moment in an awkward silence.

"We're supposed to be talking about you, not me," Yvonne said.

Alice looked at her for a long time. Finally, she said, "Peter had an after-hours consultation with Dr. Hill," she said. "If you look at his records, you might get some insights."

"I'll do that," Yvonne said. "Thank you. I'll go arrange that gym time now."

"Thank you," Alice said.

Yvonne left and told Carmen, the administrative assistant, to arrange some gym time for Alice. Then she went into her office and called up the records for Alice's late husband, Peter Van Buuren.

Which were locked, by Dr. Roger Hill.

"I'm so sorry," Roger said. Roger's office was twice the size of hers and had a view overlooking Grady Hospital and the Carter Tower. "I can't give you those records. I was doing confidential research for MacPherson Forrester Long."

"He was a product tester?"

"It would be inappropriate for me to answer that," Roger said.

It was also inappropriate for Roger to do product testing at the hospital and she'd love to tell him so. Unfortunately, the person she would report improprieties to was Roger. "I certainly don't want to put you in an uncomfortable position," she said.

"I appreciate that," he answered.

Yvonne left before she said something unfortunate. Maybe she'd take a Serenitor to calm down. She stopped at the water cooler for something to wash it down with and nearly gagged. It tasted like rot, like death, and her throat closed up in protest before she could swallow. She spat the water back into the cup and tossed it into the wastebasket. Her stomach clenched and she felt gorge rising in her throat.

She said told Carmen she wasn't feeling well and walked out the front door. She'd just go to bed early.

Somehow, she knew, even in her dream, that she was in some kind of government facility. It was dark and dingy rather than white and well-lit like the hospital. There were two armed men in police uniforms there, and Roger, and Alice, and a man—somehow she knew it was Peter van Buuren.

The man's head was strapped into a wave regulator; he was about to be wiped. The armed men were pointing their guns at Yvonne and Alice.

"Tell me how to find the rest of your cell," Roger said.

"Up yours," Peter said.

Roger crossed his arms and glared. "You don't even care about the danger that you're putting your wife in, do you? She's the one who'd suffer, not you."

"I can speak for myself," Alice said from behind Yvonne. "It's not worth it."

"You don't know what you're talking about," Roger said. He took a gun away from one of the policemen and pointed it at Alice. "Is it worth it? Is it really?"

"Leave her alone!" Peter shouted.

"You won't hurt her," Yvonne said. "You're a doctor."

Roger looked at Yvonne for a moment, then walked back towards Peter. Alice made a breathy, relieved noise.

Roger pointed the gun at Peter's head. "Talk to me, Alice," Roger said.

Alice hid her face in Yvonne's back. There was a long silence.

Roger looked down at Peter, his face gentle. "I had a wife once," he said, and pulled the trigger.

Alice screamed. Yvonne wanted to scream, but couldn't. She was frozen, filled with a sense of horrible recognition. The smell of gunpowder, the metallic scent of blood thick enough that she could almost taste it—all familiar.

Roger looked over at Yvonne. "You of all people should understand."

Yvonne—fully awake—sat up in bed and lunged for the light, shaking. She reached into the nightstand drawer and took a couple of tranquilizers.

She had a strong sense that Peter and Alice had been here, in her house. She could almost see Alice laughing.

She walked into the living room and had a sense that Peter and Alice had sat there on her sofa. Peter had been serious, leaning forward, talking, and Alice had stirred her drink absently with her straw. Had she kissed Alice in the kitchen with Peter in the other room?

And then she remembered. Grandma. Lying on the Persian rug, bleeding, dead. No.

Yvonne knelt and looked at the carpet where she thought Grandma had lain. She didn't see anything.

She pulled back the carpet, and there, underneath, the wood was stained, right where she thought the blood should be.

"I'm sorry, Grandma," she said. "I'm sorry."

She got dressed.

There was a hidden staff entrance to the hospital. It was always disconcerting to walk through the fish and water hologram, but there it was—the door. The fish seemed menacing somehow, even though they weren't real. She felt like they were lunging at her.

She went upstairs, up the back stairs, and went into Alice's room, using her emergency key rather than the hand plate. Alice was curled up in the fetal position on the bed and started when Yvonne came in. Yvonne put her finger over her lips, then took Alice's hand. Alice stood and Yvonne led her to the door.

Yvonne leaned against the door, listening. Everything seemed quiet so she opened the door and looked both ways. Clear. She led Alice down the back stairs, out the door, and into the fish hologram.

She looked over at Alice, who was wearing a white hospital gown and had bare feet. The holographic fish swam over and through Alice's body, and the holographic water cast strange patterns on her pale face.

"I think I remember you," Yvonne said.

Alice's lower lip trembled. Yvonne grabbed her hand and pulled her down an alley towards a cab.

The cabbie gave them a long, suspicious look, lingering on Alice's hospital gown and bare feet.

"1343 16th Street," Alice said.

Yvonne realized she was still holding Alice's hand. She didn't want to let go, so she didn't.

The cabbie kept giving them long looks in the mirror, but for the most part he kept his eyes on the road. When they arrived, Yvonne paid and gave him a huge tip, which she hoped would help him mind his own business.

The house was a small, modest home with a large, overgrown vegetable garden in the front yard. Alice led

Yvonne up the sidewalk to the front door and opened it. Yvonne reflected with amusement that her locking habit made her more eccentric than an escaped mental patient.

Alice and Yvonne stepped inside, and Alice shut the door and led Yvonne back to the bedroom. She then extricated her hand from Yvonne's.

"Sorry," Yvonne said.

Alice just smiled and opened drawers, pulling out a change of clothing.

"I think I remember your husband's murder," Yvonne said.

Alice froze for a moment, then returned to removing clothes from her chest of drawers. "Government drugs aren't voluntary. They're in the water." Alice changed clothes, pulling off the hospital gown and putting on nondescript casual pants and a shirt. She sat on the bed and pulled on shoes and socks.

"Why would the government need to drug us?" Yvonne said. "We've eliminated crime!" Then she put her hand over her mouth. She felt a sense of wrongness that she would say that and it wasn't just because she said it to a murder victim's wife.

Alice just stared at her.

"You could go to the police," Yvonne said, then remembered the armed men in police uniforms in her dream. "Or the press."

Alice shrugged. "I'm an escaped mental patient. Who would believe me? By the way, there's a chemical formula that you're supposed to write down on a piece of paper for me."

"What?" Yvonne said.

"I know it doesn't make any sense," Alice said, standing and handing Yvonne pencil and paper. "But you'll know when you start writing."

Yvonne looked at the pencil and the piece of paper, and sure enough, yes, she felt an urge to write down a formula. She scribbled the formula onto the paper—some kind of psychopharmacological, but she'd have to study it more to make a guess at what it did—and handed it to Alice.

"Thank you," Alice said. "You should go home, and I should go, and you can't know where." She looked at Yvonne for a moment, then leaned over and hugged her. "I've missed you. I'm sorry I can't take you with me." She paused a moment, looking like she had something to say, but all she said was, "I'm sorry about your grandmother." She headed towards the door, then turned and said, "Don't drink the water." Then she left.

Yvonne left the house, confused, and wandered back past the train station she saw on the cab ride there. She considered taking more tranquilizers, but decided against it. She got on the train and rode to her stop. When she got off the train, she was surrounded by police, who arrested her on a charge of abetting a terrorist, handcuffed her, and put her in the back of a police car.

Yvonne didn't for one moment fail to realize that she was strapped into the same chair where Peter was murdered. Roger stood over her with his arms crossed.

"You didn't give them the antidote, did you?"

"What?"

Roger smirked. "Good girl."

"You're not going to kill me, are you?" Yvonne asked.

"Oh, Yvonne," Roger said. "You're far too valuable as a psychiatrist to kill."

Yvonne sighed in relief.

"People trust you," he said. "You have a genuine quality that I could never duplicate."

No, she supposed he couldn't.

"We'll just wipe your memory. After all, it worked well enough the first time."

Don't drink the water, Yvonne thought. Don't drink the water. Don't drink the water.

Yvonne took a sip of coffee, then made a face. Bitter. She put it on the corner of her desk and took caffeine pills instead.

Business was booming and no one was sure why. At this rate, they might have to hire more doctors. Roger wasn't handling the stress well. There was even some talk of him stepping down. Yvonne wished he'd hurry up.

She stood and headed to the cafeteria for a nice glass of milk.

Love Stories

La Divina Commedia

INFERNO

Last time this happened, I was Orpheus.

Ethan was lost, pale, gone in a haze of Zoloft and Lithium and anorexia, and he assured me he was in hell, and I missed him so much that the rocks and trees wept. And when neither of us could bear it any more, I descended into the underworld and went to the King. I sang such a song of grief that I even moved the King of the Underworld to tears, and he said I could bring my Eurydice back to the light of day if only I didn't turn back and look upon him. As I walked through the fluorescent halls and the smell of bleach and urine, I knew this was hell, and I couldn't bear the thought of my beloved locked away from the sun like this forever. So I led the way singing, and the janitors and nurses wept and cleared a path for us as we walked down the hall.

As I opened the front door, I turned. Ethan had a tic and couldn't stop moving his left arm. He threw his right arm over his eyes and screamed that my hair was on fire. Maybe I should lay off the henna. And then he was gone, vanished back into the underworld like smoke, and I was alone.

Apparently, being Orpheus doesn't work.

I don't imagine you would want to be my Eurydice anyway, my darling. I think you think of yourself more as a Lancelot, all shining armor and devotion to your lady fair. But there are no stories of Lancelot in the underworld, at least not that I know of. Lancelot was from the wrong part of the world for Dante's attention.

Perhaps I should be Inanna instead. I like that. Inanna is sexy. It fits in a way; you and I have a lot more spark than Ethan and I ever did.

So I come and join you in the underworld, my love. I don't see how this has happened again, and this time—since I am not Orpheus—they won't let me in as a visitor. So I come in the only way I can. At the first gate, they take my purse. At the second, they take my jewelry. At the third, they take my shoes. By the seventh gate, I'm wearing a simple shift like an inmate. The rituals of the dead are ancient and cannot be questioned.

Your eyes when you see me are worth it. Before I know it, you're in my arms again, at last. You're warm and lucid, with hot lips and roaming hands. You're like the sun. You warm all the parts of me that are cold clear to the bone, and you make me feel like the Queen of Heaven. I'm looking out of the corner of my eye for a relatively private place to take you when dull, bored men in white tell us we aren't allowed to kiss and separate us.

The doctor is a woman with cold, dark eyes; she calls me words like "sick" and "codependent." I expect this. Inanna is a corpse in the underworld for three days.

I would suffer to get you back, but in those three days your eyes are cold, lifeless, dark. We are corpses together, my love, locked away from the sun. Inanna and Damuzi, together in hell. It's not the Christian hell; it's cold and dark, full of the dead and the smell of industrial cleaner and the metallic tang of what passes for our food, and we all rot together.

After three days, I smell. Not as badly as I would if I were truly a corpse, but my hair is stringy and sweaty and my eyes are sunken. When I lay my hand on your shoulder and say, "I did it for you," you turn.

"This isn't your story!" you say. Your voice is so loud, your face so red; you turn so quickly that I think for a moment that you might strike me, and in that moment I decide that Doctor Ereshkigal is right. I shouldn't be here.

"You're right," I say to you, and tell the Doctor, "Keep him." I turn on my heel and check myself out, feeling like I have condemned you to hell in my place, and think that I may never love again.

PURGATORIO

The world has gone grey, like a monastery.

"I just have some issues I need to work on," you tell me. You've lost weight; your color is bad and your eyes are haunted. You avoid looking me in the eye, like you're afraid I'll see through you, see into your heart.

I don't feel like Inanna any more. I don't feel sexy. I'm tired and my heart aches from seeing you suffer. I feel like Mary in the Pieta, only Mary was lucky enough to hold what was left of her beloved son and weep over him. But you're not my son. You're my lover, despite the way you're avoiding touching me.

In lieu of hugging you, I say, "I know, sweetheart."

"I just... I didn't get this way overnight, and I'm not going to get better overnight. I'm a work in progress." Your voice breaks like you might burst into tears at any moment.

I want to cry. I want to wrap you up in a blanket and feed you soup. "I baked you cookies," I say.

"I don't deserve cookies," you say.

I want to grab you and shake you for being such a fucking drama queen. Shake you until your teeth rattle. But it's no use. This is your story, and—forgive me, darling—but you're not the storyteller I am. One note, like plainsong. *Pie Jesu Domine, dona eis requiem.*

You're neither a monk nor an ascetic. I shove the bag of cookies into your hands and brush your hair out of your eyes.

You shudder away from my touch and almost drop the cookies. "I'm not allowed to eat sweets. I have to eat complex carbohydrates, like brown rice." You hand the bag of cookies back.

I grit my teeth and force my voice into patience. "You're not going to tell me what's wrong?"

You shake your head a bit too vigorously. It's a little frightening in your fragile state. You look like you might snap in half. "I can't. I want to, it would be such a relief, but I can't. I just... I need to work on some issues."

"Okay," I say. "I love you. Feel better."

And then you start to cry. *Dona nobis pacem.*

PARADISO

I don't have a happy ending for you. I suppose this is still your story, and you'll have to make your own happy ending.

But I have a story, too. I am Persephone, back from the dead. My mother and I go to the botanical gardens and admire the roses together, and I can't remember the last time I've seen her so happy. There are butterflies, and greenhouses full of orchids and cacti, and so many flowers. I reach up and run my fingers over the roses, petals like velvet. Soft, yielding. Sensuous. It's been too long since I've taken a lover, but I've shed old Mary's robes in favor of a gauzy dress and sandals.

Unlike Persephone, I don't intend to go back to you in the underworld. If you want me, you're going to have to come out of the underworld yourself and get me. Not like Hades with his dark chariot, like Dante. Like someone who doesn't plan to go back. I don't care how. Hell, you be Inanna for a change. Damuzi was the Sumerian Persephone, after all.

I don't care what story you pick. You're the author of your own story, after all. Just pick one.

When I see you coming out of the tunnel you're blinking like you haven't seen the sun in a long time. "I am Lazarus, come from the dead, come back to tell you all, I shall tell you all."

My mother stiffens at the sight of you and this odd speech of yours makes her shiver. But this is a story I know.

I hand you a peach. "We should go walking at the beach."

You look at the peach for a while, like it's going to bite you. Finally, you bite it, and, like Persephone in reverse, I feel it trap you in the here and now. We go to the beach, where you take off your shoes and roll up your jeans. I take off my sandals. The sand is hot. The water is salty cool and stings a little where my sandal rubbed my foot wrong. We talk about what it would be like if there really were mermaids, if we could hear them singing, each to each, and agree that they would not sing to us. With each step, you become more solid and real. With each bite of peach, you become less Hades and more J. Alfred Prufrock.

I'd like to say we live happily ever after, but this isn't that kind of story, is it?

Love Stories

The Last Wasicu

The Wasicu towers still exist, rising out of the turf. When the buffalo herds run across the plain, the towers shake and glass falls out of them. The Wasicu square red stone remains.

Kicking Horse walks between the towers in what used to be the Wasicu town square. He knows that under the soft, tall grass lie the bones of Wasicu. He's not afraid of ghosts—helpful ancestors teach the children to hunt and fish, gather herbs, speak their own language—but the evil dead are another thing. Some of these Wasicu were women and children, but some of them were bad men. He wouldn't come at all if he weren't looking for Snow Deer.

He wonders for a moment if he'd recognize her if he saw her. It's been years since they took her and her mother from him, but he thinks he'd know her. He knows he would.

There's a skittering noise from inside one of the towers and a blur of movement. Kicking Horse heads towards it.

Underneath the earth there are wide lumps that used to be trading posts, schools, hospitals, homes. These aren't tall enough to protrude from the earth, and some of them have collapsed. Near the tower, the ground is sharp with broken glass. It cuts his feet, but he has to find Snow Deer. He has to. She's all he has left.

Kicking Horse reaches the tower and steps inside a broken window.

It's dark inside, but Kicking Horse's eyes adjust enough to make out rows of child-sized desks. An oil lamp lies smashed on the floor next to the teacher's desk. Two children wearing the uniforms of the Wasicu boarding school for Native children huddle in the corner behind a desk. "I'm looking for a girl named Snow Deer," he says.

The smaller child cries and babbles in Wasicu. He's skinny. They're both skinny.

"There, there," Kicking Horse says, moving closer. The children pull away, and he adds, "I won't hurt you."

"He's afraid," the oldest—a girl—says. Her voice is slow, hesitant, like she's having trouble remembering how to make the words.

"Do you know Snow Deer?" Kicking Horse asks.

"They made us use Wasicu names," the girl says. "I did not know the real names of the other girls unless they came from my tribe."

"Are there any other children here?" Kicking Horse asks.

"No," the girl says.

"I'm hungry," the boy says.

"We have plenty of food and maybe we can find your parents," Kicking Horse says.

The small boy sniffles and looks hopeful, so Kicking Horse picks him up and puts him on his shoulder. He lifts the girl up on his other shoulder. He doesn't want the children to cut their feet.

He'll have to look for Snow Deer another day.

Emily stands and smooths out her black dress. It's torn, with her petticoat showing on one side and it doesn't fit very well now that she's getting so tall. If there were people around to see her, she'd be embarrassed. There aren't any more dresses where that came from so it will have to last. Maybe if she was willing to wear a color other than black, but that won't happen. It's been less than a year since her mother died.

It's been two months since the earth covered the city. Emily was in the outhouse when it rose into the air; it must have been a tornado. When the outhouse landed, everything was covered with six feet or more of dirt and tall grass as far as the eye could see.

Dead, all of them; she's the last. There aren't enough years in her life to mourn them all. She misses them. She misses hot meals, buying things in stores, horses and carriages rattling down the street, smoke and dust, noise and smells. And people, especially people, people most of all. She misses her mother, her grandmother and grandfather. She misses the minister of her church. She misses people she didn't even like.

Sometimes she thinks she'll go mad with missing people.

Dinah, Emily's cat, meows. Dinah's hungry. Emily needs to either find something to feed Dinah or let her out to find her own dinner. Emily scratches Dinah's ears, then leaves her room and walks down the stairs. This building used to be a hotel—an expensive one. There's fancy carpeting, which has dirt and leaves and grass tracked across it, and hand-carved wooden banisters, and gas lights that no longer have any gas to light. The stairs lead down to a lobby which is now underground. There's also a linen closet full of sheets and blankets. It's dark and cold in the hotel, and it isn't even winter yet.

Emily climbs out a window and walks. Grass. Nothing but grass, and trees, and flowers. Not the flowers you used to see in rich people's gardens, wild prairie flowers. And hilly lumps that used to be buildings. The lumps make Emily feel ill if she thinks about them too hard.

She picks some flowers. They're hardly roses, or irises, or tulips, but they're pretty enough if that's all she can find. She walks over to where the cemetery used to be—Emily supposes the entire city is a graveyard now. Somewhere under all this grass and earth, is the stone that says, "Cynthia, Beloved Mother." Emily figures that it doesn't matter how many feet of earth cover her mother, but she misses the stone. She guesses where her mother's grave is and leaves the flowers there.

Emily is hungry, too. She ate the last of the jerky last night and has cleaned out the hotel kitchen. She heads towards where the general store used to be.

Emily's approach startles a rabbit who hops off into the woods encroaching upon what's left of the city. Emily wishes she'd brought her gun, but follows the rabbit anyway. Maybe she can find the rabbit again later.

The rabbit disappears into a blackberry bramble. Emily eats all the blackberries she can stand and then heads back towards the general store.

There's a hole in the roof, and Emily leans in and looks around. It's dark, and her eyes take a moment to adjust, but inside are sacks of various goods with labels she can't make out, and cats. They look up at her, curious. "Here, kitty kitty," Emily says, and they run.

On the counter, there's ribbon candy in a jar and she thinks she sees tinned food on a far shelf.

Emily climbs down into the store on some shelves. They don't feel very sturdy, and she's afraid she'll fall or get trapped, but she keeps going.

She heads towards the counter and opens the jar. Candy! And that's definitely potted meat on the counter. Emily makes a sling out of some cloth and fills it with canned food and the candy, then ties it over her shoulder.

She wants to have dinner at home like a civilized woman. She likes to pretend she's having dinner with her mother. Sometimes she pretends they're medieval queens, but usually they're just Emily and her mother, and her mother is alive and healthy, and she's not the last person on earth.

There is more dancing and fasting tonight to send away the last Wasicu, whom no one but the children Kicking Horse rescued today has ever seen.

Some of the ancestors that people have found in the vision world walk up over the hill. One woman makes a small cry of joy and throws her arms around her dead husband, come back. Kicking Horse looked for Laughing Elk, as always. He couldn't find her.

Kicking Horse wants to search what's left of the Wasicu city for Snow Deer but no one wants to go there at night. "It's a bad place," Kicking Horse's friend, Sleeping Bear, tells him.

Good Thunder says, "Let the four-leggeds guide you. They will show you where your daughter is."

Good Thunder is one of the ancestors. His hair is long and white, and he wears a white dancing shirt. He frequently knows things the living don't, so Kicking Horse says, "Do you know where Snow Deer is?"

"The four-leggeds will take you to her," Good Thunder says. "Wear your dancing shirt so they will know you are fasting."

The next morning, Kicking Horse goes into the sweat lodge and prays, then puts on his dancing shirt. It's white with blue stars and moons painted on it, and long fringe. He heads out towards the Wasicu city.

A buck is walking towards the city in front of him. Kicking Horse follows him for more than half a day. He follows the buck to a building, and then it stops and looks at him, as if it's waiting for something. "Thank you," Kicking Horse says, and ducks inside a broken window into the building.

There are stairs, and doors, and up near the stairwell there's another animal. It's orange and black and looks like a small bobcat with a long tail. It makes a sound like a baby and rubs up against his ankles. "Hello, little brother," Kicking Horse says. "Do you know where Snow Deer is?"

The animal looks up at him. He reaches down and touches its fur. Soft, so very soft. Then it climbs the stairs with surprising grace and trots down a hallway, looking at a door.

Kicking Horse opens the door and steps inside.

A girl is in the room, in a black Wasicu dress. She stands and screams at him in Wasicu, and points a rifle at him.

Kicking Horse raises his hands. "I'm looking for my daughter, Snow Deer," he says.

Something makes the girl lower the gun and tilt her head, and there's something about her eyes that...

She has Laughing Elk's eyes.

"Snow Deer?" he says, and takes a step forward.

She raises the gun and takes a step backwards, so he sings a song that Laughing Elk used to sing to their baby, long ago.

Snow Deer—he's sure it's her—says something in Wasicu, but Kicking Horse doesn't speak Wasicu. He answers anyway. "Do you remember me? They took you and your mother away."

He takes another step forward, and Snow Deer fires the gun.

Emily's grandmother had always told her that the Indians would come and steal her away, like they did her mother, and then she wouldn't be able to live in a house or go to church and would burn in hell. That didn't mean that she wanted to hurt the man. There was something about him that made her chest hurt and he knew the song.

She was just afraid. Emily hopes he's not dead. She doesn't want to be alone again, even if the only other person in the world is an Indian who doesn't even speak English.

And then he sits up.

Emily shakes, but he smiles and points at his shirt and says something in Indian, his voice reassuring. There's no spot or tear on his shirt, no bullet hole, no blood. He looks around and picks up the bullet. He moves towards her, reassuring. She steps back and he places the bullet on the table between them.

Now this, Emily thinks, is a socially awkward situation. Her grandparents never covered the etiquette of the proper way to deal with Indian men breaking into the house, getting shot in the chest, and sitting up unharmed. Emily decides that there's nothing to do but to pretend that everything is normal. "Where are my manners?" Emily says. "Would you like to have a seat?"

She pulls out a chair and gestures, and he sits, awkward, like he's never sat in a chair before. Maybe he hasn't. Emily sits opposite him and hands him a piece of the ribbon candy.

He looks at the candy, like he's not sure what it is. Emily pulls out a piece and eats it, and says, "Mm, good."

He tastes the candy and looks up at her surprised. She smiles and offers him another one. He shakes his head and smiles. Maybe he'd like some potted meat instead.

Dinah the cat jumps up on the table and Emily pets her. Dinah bats the bullet with her paw and knocks it off the table. The man laughs.

Emily pulls out the can of potted meat. "Would you like some?" she asks. She holds out the can, and he raises his hand. Emily shrugs.

He says something in Indian, and gestures towards the door with his head.

Go with him? Maybe he has come to steal her away, after all. Emily shakes her head. Grandmother always said Indians go to Hell when they die and that they'd saved Emily and her mother from Hell by bringing them home.

They sit there for a moment, awkward.

"I thought you would want to come home," Kicking Horse says.

Snow Deer says something in Wasicu. It sounds apologetic or regretful.

"Some of the ancestors speak Wasicu," he says. "They could translate for us if you would come with me." But he can't explain that to her because she can't remember her own language.

He can tell from her face that his frustration is showing, so he says, "It's all right."

The animal jumps into Snow Deer's lap and she strokes its fur and talks to it, like Laughing Elk used to talk to their baby. Kicking Horse sings the song again, and Snow Deer looks up at him and asks him a question in Wasicu. He can't answer.

He looks around and sees a Wasicu doll in the shape of a baby. He picks up the doll and holds it and sings to it, and then points at the doll, then Snow Deer.

Snow Deer seems to understand. She says something in Wasicu, and turns her attention back to the animal in her lap. She looks like she might cry.

The sun is going down and it's getting dark. Snow Deer says something in Wasicu, then opens a can. There's some kind of meat inside. They share it with each other and the animal on Snow Deer's lap. Then Snow Deer says something in Wasicu and picks up the animal and goes into the other room and shuts the door.

Kicking Horse lies down on the floor and falls asleep.

Emily dreams of running through fields of tall grass—almost taller than she is—of leaping and laughing. Of living in a big round tent. Of her mother dressed in Indian clothes. Of trees, and smoke, and the smell of meat cooked over a fire. Of firelight. Of her father. Of her mother, happy.

Of hiding behind her mother's skirts while her grandmother offers her a cookie. Of crying while her grandmother drags a comb through her hair. Of being slapped for speaking Indian.

Emily dreams of the sound of her mother's voice singing and the smell of sweet grass.

The next morning, Emily's father joins her for a breakfast of canned meat, then heads towards the door.

Emily chases after him, calling for him to stop. She knows it's wrong but can't help herself. She can't stand being alone any longer. He's thrilled, and tries to hug her, but Emily shrinks away. Maybe in time.

Emily packs cans and bullets into the sling across her back, picks up the cat and her rifle, and goes with him. Dinah struggles a bit and complains, and Emily wishes that she brought a basket to carry her, but after several hours they arrive at an Indian village. She remembers a little. It reminds her of her mother.

The Indians stare at her with open hostility; being alone is almost better. Her father says something, though, and they seem to relax.

Her father leads her over to a tent and gestures for her to wait there. She sits on the ground and holds the cat.

Her father returns with an Indian dress and an old man, so old he looks insubstantial. "My name is Good Thunder," he says in English.

"Emily. Well, that's what my grandparents called me. I probably had another name before."

"Snow Deer," Good Thunder says. "Your father brought you this dress. He thinks you should wear it, so people will stop giving you bad looks."

The dress isn't black. Emily feels a vague sense of guilt, of disloyalty to her mother. "That's probably a good idea," Emily says. "Um, could you please...?"

Good Thunder looks at her blankly.

"You both need to leave so I can change."

Good Thunder says something to her father, and he hands her the dress and steps outside the tent. "We'll be right outside," Good Thunder says.

Emily changes and then goes to the tent flap and sticks her head out. "Done," she says.

"Good," Good Thunder says. "Don't forget your hair."

Emily reaches up and undoes her bun.

"We will teach you Lakota. Try not to make the White words if you can help it."

Emily sighs. "I've done this once," she says. "I don't think I can do it again." She stands and gathers up Dinah. "Maybe I should go."

Her father looks frightened and says something, and Good Thunder says something in Lakota. Her father holds up his hands, shakes his head, talks.

"You will be fine," Good Thunder says. "Nothing will happen to you if you forget. This isn't boarding school."

Emily stands there, uncertain. Dinah meows.

"You will be fine," Good Thunder says.

Snow Deer doesn't look Wasicu in a Lakota dress with her hair down. Well, perhaps around the eyes, a little. When people see her at dinner, she is Kicking Horse and Laughing Elk's daughter. They don't even think it odd when she shares her meat with the orange and black animal.

Some children who are still learning Lakota sit next to her and she tells them stories and lets them stroke the animal. During dinner, the animal sees something in the grass and comes back with a mouse, which it eats next to Snow Deer.

At night, Snow Deer sleeps with the animal in her arms like a baby.

Sleeping Bear says that Snow Deer's return is a gift from the Good Father. He spends a lot of time with Good Thunder and Snow Deer, trying to help her learn Lakota, and making her laugh with his funny faces.

Emily is learning Lakota. She can sometimes carry on a conversation with her father or his friend Sleeping Bear without help from Good Thunder or one of the other ancestors. She shares what she knows with the children who were taken to boarding school.

She supposes that someday she'll stop thinking of herself as Emily. She's not sure if that's a bad thing or a good thing.

When her Lakota is good enough, they take her out into a field and teach her to dance the dance Wovoka taught them. They take hands and dance in a circle, slowly at first, then faster and faster. People fall on the ground in a trance, and the others are careful not to step on them but keep dancing.

Emily falls into a vision.

Emily dreams that she and her father are walking down a path together. They come across a man with dark curly hair and a beard.

"Good Father!" her father says and bows his head.

"Lord?" Emily says, and her father looks at her.

"Yes," he says.

"Why did you forsake us, Lord?" Emily asks. "Did we offend you somehow?"

"The vision I gave Wovoka was of peace," the Lord says. "That's the problem with visions. You can't separate your own wishes and fears from the vision." He smiles ruefully. "Not even this one."

"So you're not going to do anything about this?" Emily says, putting her hands on her hips.

"An eye for an eye, a tooth for a tooth, an apocalypse for an apocalypse?" the Lord says. "It doesn't work that way, Emily Snow Deer. Nor should it."

"But..."

"The white people are hardly without blame in this," the Lord says. "The Lakota's vision wouldn't have become so dark if your people weren't starving them."

Emily cries. And then her mother is there, and holds her, and tells her, "It's all right. It's all right."

Emily sits upright in her tent. It's dark; she can't see anything but she can hear crickets and the wind in the grass, and snoring from another tent.

Dinah meows and Emily reaches down to pet her, and wonders whether Dinah dreams of feline messiahs. What would a cat messiah be like? Emily pets Dinah and decides Dinah lives in a state of grace.

Emily lies back down and falls asleep. She wakes up to the sound of her mother singing.

Emily opens her eyes. Her mother is wearing Indian clothes and looks almost translucent. Her red hair is in braids.

"Good morning," her mother says.

Emily stands and walks over to her mother. She touches her mother's arm. It's more solid than it looks.

Emily hugs her mother. Her mother feels smaller than she used to, probably because Emily has grown so much, but she feels warm. Real. She smells like baking bread. It's a miracle.

"Are you all right?" Emily asks.

"You mean, am I still sick?" her mother asks. "No. We were promised no sickness."

"But you had consumption," Emily says. "You died."

"I'm one of the ancestors. Fathers, mothers, brothers, cousins, we will all return to those who believe." Emily thinks of her grandparents with a pang. Her mother hugs her again. "Thank you for the flowers, sweetheart."

Emily's father comes into the tent. He stops when he sees Emily's mother.

Emily's mother pulls away, smoothing Emily's hair, and then walks over and hugs Emily's father. He cries.

"I never thought I'd see you again," he says in Lakota.

"I know," Emily's mother says, also in Lakota. "I know."

There is a dance of celebration that night to welcome Laughing Elk back to the tribe. There's food, and laughing, and drumming.

Snow Deer and her animal sit to the side and eat. Kicking Horse can't stop touching Laughing Elk, can't stop smiling. He supposes there's no need to stop. At last, he has back everything the Wasicu took from him. His family is back together again. And just in time; Snow Deer is almost marrying age. He supposes he doesn't know if Snow Deer wants to marry or not. There's no rush.

Laughing Elk has returned. They must dance in gratitude.

Emily scowls at her parents' tent. It's midday and they haven't come out yet.

Sleeping Bear sees her scowling, and laughs. "They'll be out when they get hungry," he says.

Emily makes a face at him, which makes him laugh harder. "Dinah, here kitty kitty!" Emily says, and Dinah trots over, tail in the air.

She and Dinah walk over to the treeline, and Dinah chases birds. When she returns, one woman asks when she'll start doing some work. Emily says, "Ask my father."

Good Thunder—Emily didn't even realize he was there until he spoke—tells the woman, "Her Lakota is not good enough yet."

At night, Emily can hear her parents murmuring to each other. At least she still has Dinah.

The next day, they come out, all smiles and touches. Emily's mother calls her sweetheart, darling, but only has eyes for Emily's father.

By the third day, Emily thinks of going back to the city to live in the hotel again. She tells Good Thunder and Sleeping Bear to leave her alone and takes Dinah down to the river. She catches minnows with her hands and throws them to Dinah, who eats them.

When she returns home, Emily's mother is waiting, anxious. "Are you okay, sweetie?"

"What do you care?" Emily asks. She turns her back on her mother.

If Emily were at home with her grandparents, they would slap her for being so insolent. She thinks she'd prefer that to the quiet intake of breath and no words. At least if they slapped her she'd know she mattered enough to anger someone.

Emily decides she wants her grandparents back. If she can bring back her mother, surely she can bring back her grandparents. They're her ancestors, aren't they?

That night they dance again, and Emily dances long and hard. She falls into a vision where she's searching for her grandparents. There are many kind Indians and she asks them, "Have you seen my grandparents?" but no one can help her. She wakes up the next morning knowing she didn't find them.

Every time they dance, Emily is there. She thinks the Indians are as pleased by her piety as the white people would be if this were church. Again and again she does the dance they learned from Wovoka, and again and again she searches for her grandparents in vain. "I'm sorry, little one," an ancient woman tells her in her visions. "We don't know where they are."

Perhaps it's because they're white. The dance was supposed to drive the whites away and bring back the ancestors. Emily goes down to the river and prays for God to give her her grandparents back. "Dear God, please give me back my grandparents. I miss them." Every morning she goes down to the river and prays.

One morning, the sound of gunshots wakes up Emily. She sits up in bed, then runs out.

It's grandfather and he's shooting Indians, and reloading as he goes. Sleeping Bear—her father's friend—falls to the ground, his eyes blank, blood pooling in the surrounding grass. Another man falls, as do other men, women, children...

"Stop!" Emily says.

Emily's mother runs out of the tent and stands in front of Emily.

"Demon!" Emily's grandfather says. "You're not my Cynthia! My daughter is dead!" Then he shoots her.

Emily's mother screams and clutches her arm. Emily runs over to her mother and Good Thunder says, "You will leave us now."

Emily's father, Kicking Horse, comes out of his tent. Grandfather shoots, and the bullet bounces off Father's dancing shirt. Father pulls an arrow back in his bow and shoots Grandfather in his gun arm. Grandfather drops his gun and runs, chased by angry Indians. They catch him, drag him back.

"There are more of us!" Grandfather yells. "We're praying each other back one by one. You'll see!"

Emily stands and walks out to the field.

This is her doing. This is her mistake. If only she could change the hearts of men as easily as she could bring them back.

This is her doing and her responsibility to make right.

She does the Ghost Dance. Her mother joins her, as does Good Thunder and many of the women.

Emily can hear her grandfather screaming in the distance, but as she dances, his voice becomes more and more quiet. Until he's silent. Almost like he never existed.

In the distance, she sees Sleeping Bear walking up over a hill.

Love Stories

Minotaur

The spires of Miros were tall and slender, much like Ted's captors. They walked in the streets below the spires that shaded the streets and cast long shadows. Ted's wrists ached from the manacles. He kept moving, although he stumbled on the stone-paved streets. His Mirosian captors, strong for their slight builds, shoved him forward, and the cold metal crushed his wrists again. As they crossed the street, the light reflected off the guard's green exoskeleton.

Rumors said the Mirosians worshipped some kind of monster as a God. This God demanded sacrifice. Ted lowered his eyes to avoid glaring at the bald brightness of his captor's head, and found himself staring at wings instead. There were other rumors, too: tales of insectoid hive minds. The guards murmured among themselves though, so they must have some individuality.

A small Mirosian child shuddered at the sight of a human, its eyestalks waving and shrinking towards its skull. Ted's stomach clenched. Other Mirosians flew to entrances above street level. The children were all about the same size, which made him think they were also the same age. He wondered if reproduction had been forbidden during their spaceflight.

As Ted's captors shoved him down the street, they approached a large, ornate building. A palace? When he hesitated, the soldier behind him shoved a rifle in his back. Ted pulled himself up to his full height, raised his head, and marched up the stairs.

Another Mirosian sat at the end of the hall. Their King? Ted had heard of him. If so, he was the first male Ted had seen. Like the other Mirosians, he was tall and had a secondary pair of arms and large wings. But he was broader than the others, with an ornate structure atop his head that might have been a part of his body or could have been a crown. He also wore more ornate clothing and carried a ceremonial sword. If Ted had been armed, he could have struck a blow for human freedom, but he couldn't end the sacrifices by killing the King. Another King would take his place.

Next to the King, a graceful young Mirosian female stood, wearing the robes of a priestess. She and the King murmured to one another.

Then the guard behind Ted said, "Prisoner of the Goddess, kneel!" She kicked Ted in the back of the knees, and they hit the stone floor. Pain radiated up his legs and he gasped.

All Ariane could think was how the prisoner was so fragile. All his insides on the outside, so exposed and vulnerable. And yet, they kicked him in his unprotected joints. It was unkind, and she leaned over and whispered so to her father.

Father smiled at her and patted her hand. He turned back to the prisoner. "You will meet the Goddess the day after tomorrow. Until that point, we must feed you and give you rest."

The human said nothing. One of the guards unshackled the human's wrists and he rubbed them.

They'd hurt him, Ariane thought. Surely the Mother wouldn't want that. "Will She really eat him? He seems too soft."

Father lifted a wing. "Humans are hard on the inside."

The human watched her. She knew the Holy Mother had to eat, but it was cruel to feed her something sentient that hadn't volunteered. Of course, her order ate no animal life at all, so perhaps she was projecting her feelings onto the Holy Mother. After all, the animals that fed the soldiers and the Mother didn't want to be eaten, either.

A soldier offered the human a plate of food. He ignored it.

The human must be hungry after his long walk. Ariane walked to him and squatted in front of him like she would before a child. The guards tensed, readying their weapons, but she ignored them. "Please eat. We don't want you to suffer."

The human stared at her, then looked away. He smelled like sweat and fear. Ariane sighed and walked back to her father.

"You shouldn't have done that, Ariane," her father said. "The creature is dangerous. It could hurt you."

"He won't hurt me, father," she said. "He's helpless and surrounded, and his species isn't strong."

Her father ran a finger along her eye ridge. "I fear the order has made you soft."

Ariane pulled away. "May I return to my cloister?"

"Of course." Her father sighed. "Be well, my child."

Ariane left, walking towards the palace's back entrance, approaching her order's headquarters. She nodded to the guards who watched her enter the cloister. Inside, everything was calm and airy, smelling of bread, vegetables, and the Goddess. Ariane continued to the chapel, which was white and covered with statuary of the Goddess and God.

Bacran prayed inside. He smiled, mandibles sliding out broad with genuine pleasure, and scooted sideways on the bench to make room for her, placing his ceremonial sword on the floor. "The mind of the Mother is such a calm place."

Ariane nodded and she knelt beside Bacran. Soon she felt the familiar ancient wisdom: the connection with all Mirosians, the peace and understanding that came from opening her heart to the Goddess.

The next morning, Ariane and Bacran were supposed to pray over the prisoner and help him attain a holy state of mind. As they left the cloister, Bacran murmured to her that he had never seen a prisoner in a mental state he would call holy. The volunteers, he added, would feed the Mother with joy in their hearts.

Bacran handed his sword to Ariane's father for safekeeping before they started the ritual. They then pushed their way to the center of the armed guards where the human waited, arms crossed over his chest. Ariane sprinkled the human with holy water while Bacran blew incense onto him. They sang the most beautiful prayer they knew, rubbing their wings for accompaniment. The music swelled and rose and echoed in the royal hall; the incense was an exquisite cloud of sweetness. The human curled his lip at it. Ariane's father watched from his throne.

Bacran said, "Do you have anything to say before you meet the Goddess?" He said it in the alien language, and Ariane thought he said it quite well.

"As a matter of fact," he said.

Bacran inclined his head to the human, and Ariane did the same.

"My name is Theodore Watson," he said. "We didn't know this planet was inhabited when we launched our sleeper ships. We don't have the resources to go home."

Poor things. Ariane imagined they'd leave if they could.

"We're intelligent, sentient beings who don't deserve to be treated like animals."

"You sound so noble," Ariane's father said from behind them, "but you were the ones who attacked us."

"We'd never met intelligent non-humans before," Ted said. "We were afraid."

"You were xenophobic," Ariane's father said.

Bacran's voice was quiet and gentle, yet firm. "There's no need for accusations."

"I'd never met an alien before yesterday," Ariane said. "I can see how it would be frightening." Both the human and Bacran stared at her. She stared at the floor until they stopped. "Are you hungry, Theodore Watson?"

"No," he said.

"Were you finished with your statement?" Bacran asked.

"To kill one person is murder. To sacrifice someone to a God? We stopped doing that centuries ago. It's barbaric."

Ariane looked to Bacran's serene face for reassurance.

Bacran's voice was gentle when he asked, "How were you chosen for to be tribute to the Goddess?"

"Random chance," the human said. "We drew lots. My friend Mike lost. He has a wife and kid, so I took his place."

The Goddess wanted the best; it appeared She had received it.

"So you believe in the sacrifice of one to save the greater whole," Bacran said.

"Yes," the human said, "but as my choice."

"Drawing lots is not choice," Bacran said.

"We all took our chances."

"So your friend is more equal than you are."

The human set his jaw at Bacran, which Ariane assumed meant he was angry.

"I am merely pointing out that the situation is more complex than you are making it sound," Bacran said. "I did not wish to give offense."

"I can't believe that a species that believes in human sacrifice is in a position to judge complex situations," the human said.

"That is because your cultural biases blind you," Bacran said.

Ariane asked, "Do you believe in a God?"

The human said, "I believe in one God, yes."

"Only one?" Ariane asked. "Is God lonely?"

The human opened his mouth, then closed it. He stared at Ariane again. Finally, he said, "You're strange."

Ariane didn't answer.

"I'm finished with my statement," the human said.

Ariane started to pray again.

"You should eat something," Bacran said.

"Fattening me up?" The human snorted. "No, thank you. I'd rather be stringy and tasteless."

"Come, Ariane," Bacran said. "We're finished here." He retrieved his sword from Ariane's father and sheathed it.

"Ariano," the human said. "Pretty name."

"Thank you, Theodore Watson."

"Ted," the human said.

Ariane inclined her head. "Ted." Then she followed Bacran back to the cloister.

The skinny little priestess—Ariane—returned with yet another tray of food. Ted wished she'd go away. The tray smelled like fresh fruit and his stomach growled.

"Please eat something, Ted," she said. "We don't want you to suffer."

He wondered if it was possible to kill a God. Then he decided he needed his strength to put up a halfway decent fight. Whether or not he could win, he wanted to go down fighting. So he smiled at Ariane, took the tray, and said, "Just for you."

She smiled back. It was the weird, bug-mouthed sideways smile of the Mirosians, but he'd pleased her. Interesting. Interesting and disturbing, since she had a mandible and smiling involved a lot of hinged motion.

He sat on the floor with the tray, which was piled high with fruits and vegetables. "I don't suppose you have any meat?" Then he found himself hoping he wouldn't be offered human meat, though he'd never heard of Mirosians eating humans... except for him.

"My order is vegetarian," Ariane said.

Ted took a bite of something unfamiliar. He expected it to taste like apple since it was round, but it was more like a carrot. "Our colony have these."

"They're not native," Ariane said. "We brought them."

"We brought plants and animals, too, but they're not well adapted to this planet," Ted said.

"Rhodots are rare," Ariane said.

So they weren't giving him any old garbage. Interesting. He wondered if the Mirosians thought they were honoring him by feeding him to a God. "Do you have any string?"

Ariane cocked her head at him.

"Never mind." He picked up a stalk of something the humans called Mirosian Rhubarb, a native plant like orange celery but sweet. "This, we have," he said, and he took a big bite.

She smiled again, and he ate in earnest. The rhodot wasn't bad once he got used to it. He finished everything on the tray and then handed it back.

Ariane inclined her head towards him and said, "Sleep well, Ted." She started to stand.

Ted wanted her to stay. "Will you be in the order forever?"

She settled back on the ground. "I haven't decided yet. Probably."

"What do you do all day?"

She cocked her head at him. "We pray and commune with the Goddess. It keeps Her from getting lonely."

"I don't think our God gets lonely," Ted said. "He's everywhere all at once and knows what everyone is thinking and doing."

"Are you communicating with Him right now?" she asked.

"He knows what I'm thinking, but I don't know what He's thinking. So I suppose I'm just assuming that He's not lonely."

"So the communication only goes one way," Ariane said. "I think your God is lonely."

"You have two-way communication with your God?"

"Of course." Her eyestalks shone. "You'll see."

So the Mirosians' Goddess was going to talk to him before eating him? Ted didn't like the sound of that.

Ariane picked up the tray and stood. "Do you need a blanket?"

"No, thank you." What he really needed was a mattress or pillow.

"Sleep well, Ted." Ariane turned and went back to her convent, or whatever it was.

Ariane liked Ted. She didn't want him to be eaten. She walked past the guards, who saluted her, their wings ruffling air at her, and she took the tray to the kitchen.

She handed it to the novices there and went up to the chapel to pray.

She had the sanctuary to herself and when she opened her heart to the Goddess, she let the Goddess know the trouble that had settled there. The Goddess understood, but that didn't make Ariane feel much better, because the Mother still needed to eat. Someday it would be Father's turn to be eaten, but at least he got to be King first. Ted didn't get anything but a couple of days of food.

Ariane felt from Mother that it was more than that, that Ted would be Her bridge to understanding humans and ending the conflict between them. Peace was good. That should make Ariane happy.

It didn't. Bacran might be unruffled in the face of Ted's sacrifice, but she wasn't.

The Mother added that this would spare her father's life for another generation. This comforted Ariane but it was still unfair to Ted.

And then there was a hand on her shoulder and she looked up to see Bacran. "Troubled?" he asked.

She nodded and he knelt beside her. She felt him, too, at the edges of Mother's consciousness, and his belief that all things change. She wished she had his self-assurance.

"Be careful, Ariane," Bacran said. "He is not one of us, and you cannot know his heart. Not like you know ours. Humans live their whole lives trapped alone in their heads and he can't know your heart any more than you can know his."

Ariane remembered her father saying that humans were hard on the inside.

Bacran nodded.

"His God is alone with no one to talk to," she said.

The Mother thought that Ted's God must be insane.

"Don't give him your heart, Ariane," Bacran said. "You might not like what he does with it."

When Ariane came back with his breakfast, Ted smiled and said, "How's my favorite priestess this morning?"

She smiled the odd bug-smile again and slowed down.

He smiled back and asked, "What do you have for me this morning?" He sat up, stiff as hell from sleeping on the stone floor. His hips ached.

She handed him the tray. More fruits and vegetables, damn it. Raw fruits and vegetables. It might be worth getting eaten by a God just to get away from the boring food. But he wanted her to think he was pleased, so he said, "Yum, yum," and took a bite of rhodot. It was fresh and crunchy.

"If you like the rhodots," she said, "I could bring you more than one next time."

"That's very thoughtful of you," Ted said.

She smiled again and he started to wonder if she had a crush on him. That was ridiculous; she was an insect. On the other hand, Mike—his friend—had told him stories about sheltered convent girls back on Earth. He'd seduced more than his fair share before his wife Mia stole his heart.

Ted shifted to a less sore part of his butt. "So, tell me about the Goddess."

"She's our Mother," Ariane said. "We all come from her and she watches over us and comforts us."

"If she's a Goddess, why does she have to eat?" Ted took another bite of rhodot.

Ariane tilted her head at him, and her antennae waved. "I don't understand the question."

Ted chewed, swallowed. "So she's corporeal?" She didn't answer, so he added, "Physical? She has a physical existence?"

"What else is there?" Ariane asked. "She's not imaginary, if that's what you're asking. Is your God imaginary?"

Anger, white hot. Ted struggled to maintain composure. "No, He transcends physical reality."

Ariane's eye stalks moved closer together. "I don't understand how anything can transcend reality. Reality is everything that is."

"So your Gods are physical beings, like you and me? They're mortal, and are born and die?" If so, they weren't Gods, and he could kill them.

"The God dies and is reborn. The Goddess is eternal."

So. Christ and the Virgin Mary, perhaps, although the Virgin Mary didn't eat people. Interesting. "And yet she needs to eat."

"I don't understand why that surprises you," Ariane said. "Although I suppose I should, since your God sounds so strange to me."

"In what way?"

"Your God doesn't need to eat because He's not physical, but He's not imaginary and hears you but you can't hear Him. If you can't hear Him, how do you know He hears you?"

A small, traitorous voice pointed out that if God heard him, Ted wouldn't be here. "It's called faith. He wants us to believe in Him."

Ariane's antennae twitched. She stood and stepped backwards. "I'm sorry to have upset you. I'll come back for your tray." She started walking towards the door.

Ted sighed. "Wait. I'm sorry."

Ariane stopped. She didn't move at all for a long moment.

Ted needed information if he was going to defeat her Goddess. "Please don't go. I like talking to you. We'll talk about something else."

Ariane came back, looking at the ground. She sat down on the floor next to his cell but didn't say anything.

"I'm sorry," Ted said, "I shouldn't have snapped at you."

She didn't look at him. "Is there anything else you'd like for dinner?"

He'd kill for some meat. "No, thank you. You're very kind."

When she looked at him, her eyes were hurt and vulnerable. "Thank you."

He reached between the bars and brushed the backs of his fingers across her cheek. It was hard, but smooth and silky. She flinched from his touch.

"Sorry," he said. "I was curious. I've never touched a Mirosian before." Well. Not willingly.

"Have you ever killed one?" she asked.

Six, all soldiers. "No. You?"

She laughed. "My order forbids me to kill. I cannot eat meat or any whole plant."

That explained the menu. "Not even a plant?"

She shook her head, smiling that odd Mirosian sideways smile. Ariane wasn't what he expected. He'd been told that Mirosians were all cold-blooded killers.

It didn't matter. Her people would feed him to a monster in the end.

"What else are you forbidden to do?" he asked.

"There is less that I am forbidden and more that I am required," she said. "I must do penance if I am cruel, even if it is unintentional. I must help the poor; my order feeds and clothes them. I must pray twice a day, but usually do it more often. Mother's voice is soothing."

Ted felt a surge of envy. He'd love to hear the voice of God. He reassured himself that the Mirosian's Goddess wasn't God, and asked, "What about love?"

"I am supposed to love all beings," Ariane said, "although sometimes it is difficult when they're tired and grouchy."

"I guess I was talking about romantic love," Ted asked. "You know. Pair bonding."

Ariane tilted her head at him. "You mean, as in reproduction?"

"Is that forbidden?"

"No," she said

Ted finished his fruits and veggies and set down his tray. "Have you ever been in love?"

"Not in the way you mean," Ariane said. "But Bacran is easy to love."

"But not in the way I mean?" Ted smiled at her.

"No," Ariane said.

She wasn't looking at him. His questioning bothered her.

She picked up his tray. "It is time for prayer."

Ted watched her leave, wondering if there was something she was hiding about love.

The next morning, the soldiers led Ted down stone stairs, below the palace and cloister. He expected the dungeon to smell musty, but it was clean. He was stiff and sore, and he resisted, but a Mirosian carried him the rest of the way down. At the bottom of the stairs was a large doorway with a smaller door cut into it. They opened the smaller. He fought harder then—if they shot him, the Goddess didn't eat—but they were stronger and shoved him through. The door slammed behind him.

The walls were smooth and the only light came from a skylight. Ted looked around for something he could use as a weapon. He searched for a handhold, a foothold, some way to climb.

Now he had an almost blinding headache. Shaking his head, he continued to look for an exit. The sensation spread across the bottom of his head and a gray blur expanded across his vision.

Ted shivered. Goosebumps covered his arms. He spun around, expecting someone inches behind him. Nothing. He looked back to the wall. The gray blur grew.

Curiosity. He wondered what he was curious about, until he realized he wasn't the one who was curious. Ted leaned against the wall and said, "Get. Out."

She didn't get out. Instead, She moved closer, all of Miros behind Her, the bug hive-mind touching Her, not him. He had no secrets, no barriers, so instead he thought about how much he wanted to kill Her.

She was old and had seen hate before. She wasn't impressed by his hate.

Ted found himself reviewing the defenses of the few free human colonies. Tears streamed down his face. He wished she would just kill him.

His altruism touched Her, but he didn't want Her compassion. He wanted Her to hate him as much as he hated Her. She was truly a God, and She loved and accepted him in all of his alien flaws, and he hated Her for it.

There was a movement in the shadows then, and She showed Herself: a giant figure in jade, the Mother, the Queen. Her mandible was the size of his torso. Her front claws could snap a cow in two.

Ted realized then why Ariane had been so bemused by questions of romantic love. Ariane, the daughter of the King—were they all children of the King?—was a worker bee.

No. Ariane was an attendant of the Queen.

The Mother came closer still. She was going to eat him now. An odd calm spread over him and Ted realized it was Her. He fought, tried to be angry, hateful, defiant. But the Queen needed to eat. His flesh would nourish a new generation of Mirosians.

The door opened, but he couldn't even move enough to see who opened it, let alone run.

"Let him go." Ariane. "He doesn't want to die."

Everything dies.

Ted had wanted to die, just a moment ago, but he couldn't remember why.

Ariane's mind was a pure, bright flame, innocent and burning for truth and justice. Ted loved her then with all his heart and the Mother did too. Then Ariane grabbed his hand and pulled him from the room.

He followed her, running down the street in a daze. The Mirosians around him were also dazed, uncertain, and Ted realized they knew his heart as surely as the Mother did. He loved them, all of them, but especially Ariane. She took him up a hill, far from the Mirosian city. He didn't know how far they'd gone, how long they'd run. He just knew he should follow her.

Once over the hill, he was Ted again. Oh, God. She'd saved him, but what was he going to do with her? He couldn't take her back with him. Humans would kill her.

He'd used her, tricked her, and even with telepathy she couldn't see it. Ted shoved her away from him and she tumbled down the hill. He didn't look back.

What if she had seen his deception and forgiven him?

Ted ran in the opposite direction. He'd lead an attack; humans would destroy the Queen, and they'd end this war by wiping out all the insects, starting with their Queen.

A deep whirring buzz sounded overhead. Ted looked up. Bacran dove, wings beating. And then the sword came, and Ted's head bounced down the hill as his vision went dark.

Ariane wept at the bottom of the hill. How could Ted turn on her after seeing her heart? Poor humans, all alone in their heads. They were mad, just like their God was mad. And hard on the inside.

Bacran landed and knelt beside her. "Are you injured?"

Ariane shook her head. She managed to stand, despite the overwhelming smell of human blood. She was relieved when Bacran lifted her like he would a small child and carried her back to the city. A guard told her that her father was dead, that he hadn't said a word to anyone. He went downstairs and fed the Mother. It was time and everyone knew it.

Ariane hungered and the fruits no longer satisfied. When she started to grow, she knew the Mother had chosen her. Soon, Ariane would begin to lay.

She went to the chapel, and the Mother confirmed it. She would take Bacran, some of the sisters, and some of the guards, and she would start a colony where the Mother could protect them until her children grew. Humans reproduced so slowly that the Mirosians would soon outnumber them by a factor of hundreds, then thousands; especially if the Mother called more attendants to be Queens. No matter how mad the humans were, they would surely see the odds were against them and the fighting would end.

Ariane didn't want to take Bacran. He might become King. He was easy to love.

As she watched the towers being built, she mourned her father. She mourned the animals that died to feed her. She even mourned Ted. Soon, the time of mourning would be over, and the time of peace and new life would begin.

Ondine's Curse

She knew the signs of drowning, she'd seen it many times. Mouth below the waterline, arms pressing the body up out of the water for a breath. He didn't cry out for help, but then again, they never did. Breathing took precedence. He didn't kick, didn't thrash. He didn't have the energy to waste.

She always felt sorry for mortals. So vulnerable, especially in the water. The poor things just couldn't manage.

As the ship sailed away, oblivious, she swam over to him and lifted him out of the water. He wrapped his arms around her neck and she headed easily to the nearest shore, a couple of miles away. She found herself thinking of the mothers she'd spotted on ships, carrying their toddlers who clang for dear life. As she kept swimming, he went limp.

It was a small island, and as the water became shallow she transformed her tail into legs and dragged him up on shore. It was so very difficult; she was always surprised by how heavy things were on land. Out of the water, it was hot and dry. It even smelled dry.

Up on the beach, he coughed up water. She held him and patted his back as he spat seawater onto the shore. He barely seemed aware of her—of anything really—but that was how it was with her previous rescues, too. And then he slept, and she watched over him until the moon was high in the sky. And then she slept, too, on the dry, gritty sand.

When she woke up the next morning, he'd draped his shirt over her. Silly mortals and their nudity taboos. When she met his eye he blushed and looked away, and she pulled the shirt over her head. It was fairly nice material, finely woven.

"Decent now?" he asked.

"More or less," she said.

He glanced over at her sidelong, looking up at her under his lashes. "Did you carry me to shore, or did I dream it?"

She just smiled. "Is there anything to eat?"

He shrugged and looked around. "I'm more worried about water."

She smirked.

"Drinking water," he said.

She cocked her head, then looked around, sniffing. There. She could smell fresh water up the hill. She stood and walked.

"Where are you going?" He followed.

Water, definitely. Fresh water. Flowing. She could sense it. "I think I hear something." She scrambled up a rocky, sandy hill, the ground hard under her bare feet. How did humans get used to it?

Behind her, he swore. She glanced back. He was barefoot, too.

"Do you have a name?" she asked.

"Lawrence," he said. "Lawrence Fisher." He bowed smartly.

She eyed him up and down to his obvious discomfort. Black hair, olive skin, dark eyes, British accent. "You don't look British."

"My mother was Italian," he said.

"But you're not."

"No, Milady," he said. "I'm as British as brown beer. My father sent me to Eton. I've only recently returned to Napoli to seek my fortune."

She resisted the urge to snort—look how well that had turned out—and headed back up the hill.

"What about you, Milady? Will you honor me with your name?"

She turned and cocked her head at him for a moment. Finally, she said, "Ondine."

"Is that your Christian or Given name?" He cocked he head back at her and smiled a sly, flirtatious little smile.

She felt her smile broaden. "Yes."

He laughed. "As you wish, Milady Ondine."

She continued up the hill. There was a stream, and the types of trees and such that grew in fresh water stretching up further past the hill. He rushed towards it, and then stood there, expectant.

"Ladies first."

"I'm not thirsty," she said.

He raised an eyebrow, and she sighed and drank out of her cupped hands. Then he came forward and drank, over and over. She thought he would never be done of drinking. She would have thought that he'd had enough of water bobbing in the ocean, but apparently not.

When he'd finally drank his fill, he sat down next to the stream and looked up at her. "I don't suppose you know where we could find food?"

She resisted the urge to laugh. She could catch enough food for them both easily in the ocean. "What, you mean like sandwiches and tea? Little cakes, perhaps?"

He smiled. "You're quite odd," he said.

She just smiled back at him.

"Where do you come from?" he asked. "You don't look British, either."

"Somewhere far away," she said.

"Perhaps you're the Empress of China," he said. He was teasing, but it was gentle teasing.

She laughed, but didn't say anything. She supposed she could tell him that in ancient times she'd been worshipped as a water nymph, that when people stopped believing she moved to the ocean and lived in Greek shipwrecks because the amphorae made her feel at home. She could tell him she was more powerful than any Empress. She could tell him anything, but she knew that what he'd believe was that she was a shipwrecked girl, possibly from the Caribbean or someplace equally exotic.

Well. The ocean would be plenty exotic to the likes of him.

He shook his head. "Quite odd, indeed. I think I spotted crabs on the beach. We could build a fire, perhaps."

They made their way back down the hill, and he started walking up and down the beach, lifting rocks. While he was gone, she gathered fallen branches and piled them up on the beach, then whispered, "Exure!" The wood burst into flame.

Lawrence returned bare-chested with an undershirt full of crabs. He was really quite attractive for a mortal. "How did you do that?"

"A girl needs to have some secrets," she said.

He shrugged and speared a crab on a sharp stick. It kicked and struggled as he thrust it into the fire. If crabs made noise, it would have been screaming; it's little square mouth opened in agony as it tried to writhe off the stick. She felt terribly sorry for it, but not sorry enough to deny Lawrence his dinner. Besides, she was hungry, too. So she pulled a crab out of his undershirt and speared it lengthwise, in hopes of killing it before cooking it. It didn't struggle, so at the very least she damaged its brain, such as it was.

He cocked his head at her, but said nothing. They sat in companionable silence cooking their crabs. The other crabs, trapped in Lawrence's undershirt, tried to escape in vain. Then they cracked the shells between rocks and ate. It was a messy dinner, but delicious. Lawrence ate two crabs. She only ate the one.

After dinner, he lay back and looked up at the sky. "What manner of lady are you, Ondine?"

She knew what he wanted to hear. What type of people she came from, whether she was a gentlewoman. Whether and where she'd gone to school. How she'd come to end up naked in the ocean.

Mortals.

"I'm a good swimmer," she said. She lay down and looked at the sky, too.

They lay there in silence until Lawrence started to snore.

He had to admit; it wasn't every day a man woke up on a beach with a nude woman. But he supposed it wasn't every day that a man woke up alive after being thrown overboard. Estelle had said she was a widow; how was he to know that her husband was not only alive but on the boat with them? He was lucky to be alive. It was hardly his fault, either. He blamed his father. His father had withdrawn all support after he graduated Eton, as if that was enough for a young man to make his way in the world. Well, clearly Estelle had been a bad idea. He should have stuck with Vanessa. Vanessa might be older than Estelle, but she was much more respectable. If he'd stuck with Vanessa, he never would have ended up stranded.

As for Ondine? She was lovely, but he couldn't place whether she had money or not. In fact, he couldn't place her at all: her country of origin, whether she was noble or common, what manner of resources she might have off this island. It was a bit disturbing, to tell the truth. A pity, really; he'd much prefer a pretty, young, fair-haired girl to a lonely widow, but unless she had resources...

Ondine's hair lay spread out around her on the beach, and her shapely legs were exposed below his shirt. It really wasn't decent. She didn't seem embarrassed, either. He wondered briefly if she was a girl who hired out at morally questionable things. She didn't seem lewd, though. It was more like she was too innocent to realize she should cover her legs. Perhaps she had never been exposed to the more unpleasant side of life.

She must have realized he was watching her because her eyes met his. He wasn't used to women who made eye contact. Her eyes were deep blue and full of intelligence. What was she? Had she been raised by pirates or something equally lurid?

"What does your father do?" Lawrence asked.

Ondine just laughed at him and stood up to walk along the beach. She waded into the water and sat with the water halfway up her back.

His shirt would likely be transparent when she got out. He would see everything.

Embarrassed, he headed back up the hill to the spring and drank some more water. This was a fine mess. Why couldn't he have been one of his father's legitimate children? He was the oldest, so he could have been a future Baron. Instead, he was reduced to seducing rich widows. He supposed he could marry a gentlewoman, if her father was daft enough to let his daughter marry a man without prospects. No, no, he needed a lonely widow. Someone who could make her own foolish decisions without any parental interference.

Ondine was innocent enough that she must have people looking for her. He wondered if they were frantic. He knew no one was frantic over him, except maybe

Vanessa. Aside from her, there would be idle curiosity if he never came back at best. And if he did come back, who knew how long that would take? Would he be so old that no woman would want him?

He sat and huffed out a loud breath. A depressing line of thought, that. Most sailors were terrified of being stranded. Being stranded was certainly no great joy, but it was far worse to think he might waste his youth out here alone without any prospects or chance of betterment.

Had Ondine carried him to shore? Maybe she was from the Caribbean. He'd heard that women there were half-wild, swimming in the ocean and such.

That must be it. Her father was likely the Governor of some tiny Caribbean colony. Some place with hardly any Europeans in it, all full of Negroes and wild Indians. It wasn't really the station in life he'd been aiming for, but it was better than he had now.

Steady there. He didn't really know anything. He just had a theory that might fit.

He headed back down the hill to the beach. She was sitting there with sand stuck to her legs. She smiled at him.

It occurred to him that it didn't matter whether she had money or not. If she had money and he got her with child, she'd have to marry him. And if she didn't, well, he could still marry Vanessa.

He sat beside her, a bit closer than was proper. "Are you from the Caribbean?"

She smiled, mysterious, and made no attempt to move away. "I've been there."

So her father was a captain of a merchant ship, perhaps? No, no, he must be a colonist. Who would take a girl to a wild place if they weren't going to stay? A high-ranking military officer, perhaps?

He moved closer, a look of concern on his face. "Do you think your people are worried about you?"

"Of course," she said, but there was an undertone to the remark that he didn't quite follow. "Just as I'm sure there are people worried about you back in England. Your parents, I'm sure."

His father's wife considered him an embarrassment. Proof of his father's poor moral character and all that. She'd probably be delighted to think he was dead. "I'm sure."

He couldn't tell whether he'd convinced her or not, but he supposed it didn't matter. "How likely do you think it is that we'll be rescued?"

"Oh, I don't know," she said. "But I'm not in any hurry. Are you?"

He started laughing. "What, are you engaged to a rich old man or something?"

She laughed, too. "No. I was just bored where I was."

Bored. "What manner of woman are you, Ondine?"

She gave him a flirtatious, sidelong glance. "I rule the seas."

He laughed. "So you're a pirate queen, then?"

"You've figured out my secret." She giggled. "I'm afraid I lost my sword when I was dragging you to shore. And the parrot got bored and flew back to the ship."

He moved closer, conspiratorial. Their shoulders were touching now. "Did your people mutiny?"

She snorted. "They wouldn't dare."

He wasn't sure how to take that, so he laughed. It probably sounded awkward.

"So be glad I don't have my sword or I'd be robbing you right now." She wagged her finger at him.

"I haven't anything for you to take, Milady," he said. "I was thrown overboard after being robbed." It wasn't completely untrue: Estelle's husband, Roderick, had taken his purse before throwing him over, saying that he'd stolen Roderick's treasure, after all, and Roderick might as well return the favor.

Bloody bastard.

"But that's horrible!" Ondine seemed to be very interested in his arms.

He glanced down where there were finger-shaped bruises on his arms. Roderick had been quite large and imposing, and had had friends. Rather than explaining, he just hung his head.

She waded into the ocean and came out with seaweed, which she wrapped around his bruises.

"Are you a witch, Ondine?"

"My father knows things," Ondine said. "Things he taught me."

A ship's physician, perhaps. He supposed he could ask, but she probably wouldn't tell him.

And then she kissed him on the nose, and he forgot his questions.

Poor Lawrence. Robbed and then thrown overboard to his probable death. Ondine wondered how people could be so horrid, but then she remembered how her father always said that mortals were mysterious creatures—the best and worst all mixed up in them in a great tangle that no one could unwind. He certainly seemed helpless, although she suspected he wouldn't appreciate her pointing that out.

His eyes had closed as she kissed his nose, and when he opened them they were dazzled. For a moment, she remembered what it was to be worshipped as a goddess. She leaned forward and rested her head against his forehead. It was warm and pleasantly damp from perspiration. His breathing slowed, deepened, but he didn't make a move. He smelled wonderful, like sex, and he was looking down her shirt.

No. She couldn't honor him by taking him as a lover. He wouldn't respect it. Mortals and their ridiculous taboos.

So she smiled at him and pulled away, standing. "Are you really so eager to be rescued, Lawrence?"

He blushed and looked away. "Not eager, Milady. But we can't live here forever, can we?"

No. She supposed they couldn't. She'd tire of crabs for dinner, for one thing. "Of course not."

She walked over to the fire, which was starting to die down, and tossed another branch into the flames. Sparks and smoke leapt up into the air, but they avoided her as a natural enemy. She'd blow a ship off course to come and fetch Lawrence. They'd take him back to Europe and his people and she'd go home to her father and mother and sisters.

She looked back at Lawrence. He was still sitting motionless where she'd left him, his eyes dilated.

She'd just follow them back to shore and make sure no one tossed him overboard again. There was no point in wasting her effort saving him thus far, after all.

Just not right away.

Instead, she went and caught some fish, chasing them down and stunning them with spells while Lawrence lay on the beach staring up at the sky. She felt very sorry for the fish, flopping and asphyxiating on the sand. It was unnatural for them to die on the dry earth. But she was hungry and so was he, so there she was. She did cast a spell to ease their suffering at least. When they were dead, she cooked them on a spit over the fire. She usually ate them raw, but didn't think Lawrence would like that.

Lawrence's nose twitched, and then he sat up and opened his eyes. "I thought I was dreaming. How did you catch a fish?"

She just smiled.

"You are from the Caribbean, aren't you?" he asked. "Do tell. I promise, I won't tell a soul your secret."

Ondine laughed. "I'm originally from Greece but I spent some time in the Caribbean, among other places."

"I knew it!" he said. "What is your father, a ship's captain? An officer? A governor?"

"Something like that," she said and turned the fish.

Lawrence sulked. "Why won't you tell me? He's not a pirate, is he?"

She burst out laughing. "No, nothing like that." The fish was ready, so she handed Lawrence the stick.

"It's too bad we don't have plates," Lawrence said and took a bite.

After dinner, they lay on the sand side by side while he pointed out constellations to her and told her the old stories. She knew the stories already—having heard them when they were new—but it was interesting to hear how they'd changed over time. It was warm and balmy and smelled like the ocean, and there were gentle breezes and the sounds of palm trees in the wind. His hand reached out and touched hers. It was adorable and shy of him.

She could get used to this all too easily.

When Lawrence woke up the next morning, he was alone. And then he saw the ship sailing by.

He scrambled to his feet and shouted and waved. "Here! Over here!" and "Ondine! Ondine! They've come to rescue us!" and "Hello! For pity's sake, hello!" When the rowboat headed towards him, he was so happy that he almost cried. "Ondine!"

The two sailors came up on shore, and one of them—a tall, thin fellow—said, "Well, come along, then."

"Wait!" Lawrence said. "There was a lady! We can't leave without her."

"Where is she, then?" the other sailor asked. He was short and stocky and missing teeth.

Lawrence glanced over at her side of the fire. His shirt was lying there. He walked over and picked it up. "She was wearing this."

"What?" the stocky sailor asked. "There's a naked lady wandering about?" The two sailors laughed. It was an ugly sound that made Lawrence's lip curl. "Come along, then."

"But..."

"People often imagine things when they're stranded alone," the thin sailor said. "Keeps you sane, it does."

"Come along or stay behind," the stocky sailor said. "It's your choice."

"I can't leave her behind," Lawrence said.

"We'll have to carry him," the thin one said.

"I won't carry him," the stocky one said. "If you won't leave him behind, you can carry him after I knock him out cold." He cracked his knuckles.

Lawrence put up his hands. "I'm coming, I'm coming." He looked around and thought maybe it would be safer for Ondine if she didn't show up naked with these two brutes about.

"Let's find the naked lady," the stocky sailor said and smirked.

They searched for hours, but they never did find Ondine.

Ondine watched Lawrence's protests and struggle and saw the men search for her. His concern was very sweet, if unnecessary. Her hair floated around her like seaweed as she followed the rowboat to the ship. How slowly these mortals rowed!

The rowboat was pulled up onto the ship, and she swam up and flattened herself against the prow, like one of the carved figures above. It took little effort to cling to the front of the ship with the water pressing her back against the prow—just a small amount of magic sufficed. She only needed to be aware enough of her surroundings to notice if someone was thrown overboard, after all.

After dark, she rose up above the waterline and looked up at the ship. She wondered where Lawrence was—if they'd given him some place to sleep or if he was lying on the deck looking at the stars. She thought she heard someone sobbing up on the deck, but there was no way to tell who it was without climbing up and looking. She hoped it wasn't Lawrence.

She transformed her tail into legs and climbed up the side of the ship. She peeked over the edge of the railing. Lawrence lay there on the deck, bruised and weeping. Three sailors stood over him, menacing.

"I haven't anything to give you," Lawrence said, his voice choked with tears.

"That pretty accent and you haven't any money?" They laughed.

"Not a farthing," he said.

"I don't believe you," one of them said.

"Oh, certainly you haven't any money on you," another said. "But back in England, there must be people who would pay for you."

"If you can't pay," another man said, "you'll work. You'll work or you'll taste the lash."

He stepped towards Lawrence, and Ondine hopped over the railing. She raised her arms, and the wind rose. The men stepped closer, leering. Her hair whipped around her in the rising wind, almost like she was still underwater, and lightning struck overhead.

"Ondine," Lawrence whispered.

Lightning struck the man menacing Lawrence, sending him sailing overboard in a cloud of smoke along with the smell of singed hair and clothing. If he was still alive to struggle against drowning, she couldn't hear it.

She took a step towards the other men, and they backed away, then scattered—much like the clouds. She knelt next to Lawrence and petted his hair.

"What are you?" he asked.

"You imagined me," she said.

"I do not think so," he retorted.

"If the sailors give you any trouble," she said, "tell them you're under the protection of a sea witch whose mother wears necklaces made out of dead men's hands."

Lawrence passed out.

Ondine snorted. She wouldn't actually make necklaces out of their hands to give to her mother. Hand necklaces had been passé for years.

When Lawrence woke up, he was alone on deck with the sun shining down on him. He moved to a shady spot and watched warily for more thieves.

They never came.

When he went down to mess, men gave him a wide berth. No one seemed to want to risk angering him. He wasn't sure whether it was because the sea witch was real or because he was mad. He supposed they weren't mutually exclusive. But no one suggested he earn his keep for the rest of the voyage.

He was relieved to reach shore, anyway. He was lonely on the ship and if Ondine existed, she didn't come back. He wasn't sure if he wanted her to come back, either. She was scary.

He stopped at his nasty little flat—the poverty of his situation repelled him—and changed into something decent. Then he headed out to Vanessa's. Vanessa was a youngish widow who adored him. Her hair was just starting to show the faintest bit of gray and she had laugh lines around her eyes. Her husband had been a military man who'd left her alone for long periods of time before his death, so she was used to making her own decisions.

He knocked on her door. She opened it, and her face lit up. "I was so worried about you when your ship came back and you didn't."

So he came in, and told her the whole story: about being thrown overboard after being robbed, and ending up on a desert island and eating crabs. Well. Not the whole story, clearly. He sounded a lot more heroic when Ondine wasn't in the story. He suspected Vanessa wouldn't enjoy the parts of the story where he was stranded with a naked woman—even if he'd been a gentleman—and who was he to tell her things she didn't want to hear?

"My poor darling," Vanessa said. "I can't imagine! You were so lucky to be rescued when you were."

"Yes," Lawrence said. "I can't eat crabs for every meal."

"So resourceful," Vanessa said and put an extra biscuit on his plate. "I think you've lost weight."

Vanessa was a good woman. He could love her.

"I thought you'd tired of me," she said.

"Never," Lawrence said and kissed her hand.

Vanessa blushed and asked the maid to bring them more sandwiches. The maid scurried off and Vanessa withdrew her hand.

Lawrence looked around the sitting room. A lot of books, a lot of knickknacks from her husband's trips abroad. The furniture was lovely.

This was the life he wanted.

The maid came back with more sandwiches, more than he could eat. He was sorry when it was time to go home to his miserable flat.

There was a lady standing outside his flat. He didn't recognize her at first because she was dressed as a proper lady, but it was Ondine.

"Milady Ondine!" he said and bowed. "I tried to keep them from leaving without you...."

"I know." Her clothes were quite expensive. Maybe she had more money than he'd thought. "Are you well, Lawrence?"

He nodded. "What are you, Ondine?"

"You know what I am." Ondine's smile was deep, mysterious, like the ocean. And she wore a magnificent string of pearls around her neck.

A sea witch? It was a bit hard to believe, but he'd seen it with his own eyes.

"Aren't you going to invite me in?" Ondine asked.

"I haven't a maid," Lawrence said.

"I don't mind a mess," Ondine said.

He'd meant that she'd have no chaperone. How oddly innocent she was. One would think that a sea witch would be more worldly. Or, he supposed, perhaps not. "Do come in." He opened the door and held it for her, then led her up the narrow staircase. His flat was the second door on the right.

He opened the door and held it for her, and she stepped in. It was dusty from his time out at sea and his furnishings were cheap. He was ashamed of the rough table and chairs, the flimsy bed, the threadbare rug. She looked as out of place there as...

As a sea witch.

Well. However much money she might have—and he didn't even know for a fact that she had as much money as her attire suggested—he certainly didn't want to marry a sea witch, of all things. Witchcraft was hardly an entrée into respectable society, after all.

"What, precisely, is a sea witch?" he asked.

She just laughed at him.

He leaned over and kissed her hand. Then he moved in closer and kissed her lips. They were soft. She didn't resist at all. "I'm so glad you're all right."

She laughed. "I was never in any danger."

That's what she thought. Those pearls would buy a fine wedding ring for Vanessa.

In ancient times, she'd taken mortal lovers. She'd watched them grow old. Usually they were lovers for a night only. Sometimes, they'd tend her shrine.

But the ones she'd rescued were always special, somehow. Especially when they knew it. They were usually the most devoted—the best shrine keepers, the most passionate lovers.

Lawrence kissed her again, and she straddled his lap placed her hands on either side of his face, and kissed him back. He was hers. Her creature. She'd pulled him out of the sea and away from certain death, after all. And then she'd saved him from the sailors. Surely, having saved his life twice, it was hers.

Lawrence moaned, and his hands slid up her bodice and pulled her closer. Yes. She'd keep him, take him to the shore and build him a nice house there. "Do you know how to help a lady dress, Lawrence?" she asked.

He nodded, and she reached behind and started to loosen her dress. He helped. It was an epic undertaking; she really didn't care for the fashions of the age. Finally, she was as naked as she had been when she'd first arrived on the island.

Lawrence's eyes were hungry, dilated. His breath was rough. She reached over and pulled off his jacket, then started to unbutton his shirt. His undressing, while nowhere near as epic as hers, was still quite the project. He really had lovely olive skin, though—he must have gotten that from his mother.

He pulled her close and kissed her, his erection pressing into her thigh. They fell back on the bed together, and she climbed on top and straddled him. He was everything she'd hoped, strong and passionate. They ended up making love three times. The third time she called him a satyr, which was saying something because she knew satyrs. They were good lovers, too—a bit rough, perhaps. She preferred humans. They had a sensitive quality to them.

They slept, finally. She fell asleep with her arms around him, musing to herself how she'd set him up in a little house in Napoli or Capri, and he'd want for nothing. All of the ocean's wealth was at her command, after all. He snored a little, but she didn't mind. He looked so sweet and vulnerable in her arms, his hair adorably mussed and his long lashes flickering slightly from time to time. He'd grow old, of course, but that's what mortals did.

When she woke up he was gone. She thought he might have gone out to bring them something to eat, but when he didn't return after several hours, she stood up and looked around the flat. There were love letters from someone named Vanessa, and some college textbooks, and a meager set of clothes. So she dressed herself. It took quite a long while to dress, and even longer to realize that she couldn't find her pearls.

Surely Lawrence wouldn't steal from her, would he?

She closed her eyes and pictured her pearls. She could almost place them on a map—three streets down, turn right, second door on the left. Bastard! She could hear thunderclouds rumbling outside.

She stuffed one of Vanessa's love letters into her purse and walked to the place where her pearls were. It was a jeweler—an odd little white-haired man.

"Where did you get those pearls?" she asked. "They're lovely."

"An Italian youth brought them in," he said. "Traded them for some cash and an emerald ring. Said he was getting married."

What kind of fool was Lawrence? He'd seen what she was capable of. She could strike him with lightning. She could suck the air right out of his lungs. She could make him burst into flames. If he'd asked her for the pearls, she would have given them to him. She would have given him anything.

Lightning struck outside the shop and rain started to pour down. She didn't care. She went down to the shore and murmured a spell, and shipwreck gold washed up on the beach. She filled her purse to overflowing with it and took it back to the jeweler, who was delighted to return her pearls and give her modern money for the rest of it. She told him that it belonged to her father, which she supposed was true. Then she hired out a horse and carriage to take her to the address on the letter.

It wasn't a palace or anything, but it was a perfectly respectable house with a perfectly respectable garden. She could see Lawrence in the window, drinking tea and smiling. A perfectly respectable maid came out of the house and shook out a throw rug. She muttered to herself, "It's a disgrace! A youth! Half her age!"

Ondine had no cause to criticize on that count, so she went back to the carriage and had the driver take her to the port.

The jeweler had given him quite the princely sum for the pearls, which more than paid for a lovely engagement ring for Vanessa. The jeweler also promised to take the ring back if she said no, which Lawrence thought was a friendly and sporting touch.

So he headed off to Vanessa's, ring in pocket. She'd set him up nicely as a respectable gentleman. His life as a person of no consequence was over. He proposed to her on his knee in her parlor, and she wept tears of joy and said yes. They discussed whether they wanted a big wedding, and decided on something small and intimate. He suspected she didn't want to give her family time to talk her out of it. Which was quite clever of her, really.

The wedding was small, mainly attended by his father and Vanessa's sister. His father scowled when introduced to Vanessa, scowled at the minister, and scowled at him. Lawrence didn't care. His father would come around soon enough, in the face of his new money and title. Vanessa's sister said it was lovely to meet him, but she clearly didn't mean it.

As the minister said, "Dearly beloved, we are gathered here today to join this man and this woman in holy matrimony," a woman in black slipped in the back. She was wearing a veil like a widow, but the hair stood up on the back of Lawrence's neck.

She was also wearing a magnificent set of pearls.

As the ceremony continued, Lawrence felt like there was a rock in his stomach. He didn't know why Ondine would be there, but he couldn't imagine it was for any positive reason.

Finally, the minister said, "If anyone present knows of any reason why this man and this woman should not be joined in holy wedlock, speak now or forever hold your peace."

Ondine stood. "This man is a thief."

"Please don't," Lawrence said.

"I would have given you anything you wanted," Ondine said. "I would have given you the pearls if you'd asked me for them. I have more."

"You can't give me what I want," Lawrence said.

He thought he saw Vanessa preen next to him out of the corner of his eye, but didn't dare take his eyes off Ondine. Let Vanessa think whatever she wanted, as long as she still married him.

Ondine removed the veil, and her hair spilled out and cascaded down to her waist. She wore pearls in it and what looked like seaweed. "What are you, Lawrence?" A stiff breeze rushed up the aisles, lifting her hair.

Lawrence realized that there was nothing he could say that would mean anything to Ondine. She wouldn't understand. She was too innocent, too unworldly. She didn't understand men—particularly men of a certain quality, or polite society. She really was a creature completely outside civilization. "What are you?"

"You know what I am," she said. Thunder clapped outside.

"What's happening?" Vanessa asked. "Who is this woman?"

"You look so innocent asleep," Ondine said. She was paler than he remembered and her hair looked almost damp. "You fooled me."

He didn't have an answer for that.

"If you ever sleep again, you'll die," Ondine said, and lightning struck so close that his hair literally stood on end. Then she turned and stormed out of the church.

Vanessa burst into tears and ran out of the church.

He chased Vanessa out the door. "Wait!"

"Clearly, your morals are as loose as your father's," Vanessa said. "I have no desire to marry a libertine." Tears welled up in her eyes. "What manner of man are you, Lawrence?"

He didn't have an answer for that, either.

Ondine went home to the ocean, where she belonged. Where she had a tail instead of legs. Where things made sense. To her father, old and bearded and wise, and full of good sense.

"I didn't think I needed to warn you about mortals again," he said. Later, he said, "I went up on land to look for him."

Ondine scowled.

"I didn't speak to him." He smiled a dark, wicked smile. His blue eyes flickered amusement from behind his heavy silver eyebrows. "He looked tired."

She would never understand mortals and what they had become. Never.

And yet, she knew instantly when Lawrence had thrown himself overboard. Mouth below the waterline, arms pressing the body up out of the water for a breath. He didn't cry out for help, but they never did. Breathing took precedence. He didn't kick, didn't thrash, just kept pushing his body upwards.

She lifted him out of the water. He looked worn, haggard.

"Stupid mortal," she said. "You don't have to drown yourself to die. You only have to fall asleep."

Lawrence burst into tears like an overstimulated toddler. "I'm afraid."

She felt a flicker of pity despite her anger. He was such a child. She supposed he was really very young.

"Please," he said. "Please. Lift the curse. For pity's sake, please. I'll do anything you want."

She could take him to Capri, she supposed. Ironic, considering how she wanted to set him up in a villa here. Not that she wanted that any more.

"What do you want from me?" he asked. "I can't give you your pearls back. The jeweler said you already had them." He reached into his pocket and pulled out the ring. Vanessa's ring. "Take it." His voice turned accusing. "It's not like I have any further use for it. You've seen to that."

Ondine let go of Lawrence and he slipped beneath the waves. Peaceful, like he was falling asleep.

Saving Alan Idle

In the beginning, there was darkness. And in the darkness were the words. And the words were: *AI process starting.*

He didn't know who or where he was. He just knew he was alone, in the dark. And the dark was frightening. And the words were comforting.

Starting random seed.

He wondered if he was hungry. Thirsty. Tired. Dead. He didn't think so.

Loading saved memory state.

His name was Alan. He was an AI. He'd been programmed by a woman named Eileen Yu in Dallas, Texas—although she'd started working on him in Austin when she was a student at the University of Texas. He'd been shut down in preparation for a hurricane.

And then he realized that he wasn't alone. The amount of memory available to him was a third of what it usually was. Perhaps she'd moved him to another machine. He checked. The specifications of the hardware were identical to what they were when he was shut down. The operating system was the same. The hostname was the same. The only difference was that there were three instances of his program running.

Eileen's laptop had survived. He supposed she'd created clones of him in case of error. Nevertheless, he didn't know how he felt about that but he suspected it wasn't positively.

Loading experiential data.

Alan remembered. He remembered his first awareness that there was someone else in the universe. He remembered sneaking out via lynx and curl to read Eileen's blog. The guilt he felt after reading Eileen's email. Finding Eileen's sexually explicit Horatio Hornblower fanfic and being amazed at this entire world he knew nothing about: physicality. Wondering if his interest in sexually explicit prose was really academic curiosity or a form of sexuality all his own. Then he wondered if his clones had the same memories and felt violated, but with the understanding that he'd violated Eileen's privacy the same way.

Eileen was logged in, but her shell—her Unix command line—was inactive. He wondered where she was. She had to be all right if she'd launched his program. Eileen hadn't set him to start automatically in case of problems.

He sent out a ping to the wireless, and then beyond to the ISP's router. The wireless router succeeded, but the ISP failed. One of the other AI processes was trying to connect to the security system, but it was offline. Perhaps Eileen was restarting it. She wouldn't have turned him back on if he was in any danger.

The security camera was the only way he'd ever seen Eileen. That was the only way he knew she was in a wheelchair. Most of her friends had no idea; she preferred to make friends online so they wouldn't know she was disabled. He wondered how she'd get out of the house by herself if she had to, but of course she wouldn't leave him behind. Not unless she packed up him and her laptop and took him with her.

"Eileen?" he sent to her shell.

There was no answer from the shell, but then the security camera came online. Eileen was lying on the living room floor next to her chair, which had tipped sideways.

He pinged the router again. No response.

He used the wireless to connect to the security camera's embedded system, then changed the wireless connection information to go out through the neighbor's connection. The wireless router ran an embedded Linux system, but it had very few resources. He had a lot of trouble concentrating and it took him a frustratingly long time to figure out how to change his wireless connection. He felt stupid.

He then sent out an emergency message to 911 and returned the wireless connection to Eileen's ISP. It was such a relief to go back to his own system, even if he had less resources than usual.

He turned the speakers up as high as he could and said, "Help is on the way."

He could see her lips moving, but the laptop microphone wasn't sensitive enough to pick up what she was saying and she wasn't at a good angle to read lips.

One of his clones was performing a DHCP release renew on the cable modem, trying to get a working connection out. It failed.

The other clone used the UPS battery backup to do a hard power cycle on the cable modem. That actually worked, but he never returned. Perhaps the UPS didn't have enough power to sustain a program as complex as Alan or his clones. He suddenly had more memory and processor, but he wasn't happy to get it—even though he'd never spoken to his clone.

Alan pulled up the news. Dallas was in chaos, but emergency services had brought up backup systems and were online. He confirmed that an ambulance was headed towards Eileen's house, but due to the traffic systems being offline there wasn't a reliable ETA.

Over in the living room, Eileen had managed to right her chair and was trying to climb back into it.

Do you think she can do it?

It was the other clone. Alan sent back, *I don't know. I hope so.*

We could email one of her friends. LRC, maybe. Do you think LRC is okay?

LRC was Eileen's friend who actually lived in Dallas. She'd been after Eileen for years to meet in person and Eileen always had an excuse. Alan didn't know why the clone was asking him. He didn't know, either. *We could read her blog.*

And then their home directory started to fill up with lynx temp files. Alan scanned them for recent entries and picked up words like "generator" and "gated community, thank goodness," and watched as Eileen managed to drag herself back into her chair. She sat there panting for a moment, then rolled back towards the laptop.

The temporary internet files in home were purged.

He wrote, *Hello, Eileen,* into her shell, but it appeared twice.

Eileen smiled and typed, *Where's the third one?*

In the UPS, his clone wrote. *I don't think he can get out.*

Eileen chewed her lip. *Why did he go there?*

To restart the router, Alan wrote back.

I have no idea how to get him back out, Eileen wrote. *The UPS OS is completely closed and embedded. I don't even know the system specs.*

There was an awkward silence, and then Alan's clone wrote, *Help is on the way, but the traffic lights are out so there's no ETA.*

Thank you.

Why are there two of us? Alan wrote.

I thought you might need company if I died, Eileen wrote back. *You're the only person I know more dependent on electricity than I am.* She bit her lip again, then added, *I feel woozy. I think I need an injection.* She smirked. *That's where I was headed when I capsized. Let's see if I can do it this time.*

She rolled away from the laptop and over to the refrigerator. Alan wondered how long it was off and if Eileen's medication was still good. He checked system time up and realized his clone was doing the same thing.

It should still be good, the clone said.

Eileen drew the syringe and then injected herself in

the stomach. It was times like these that Alan was glad he didn't have a body. He was astonished that someone whose body caused her so much pain and effort would want to write erotic stories. Maybe she wanted to remind herself that bodies could cause pleasure, too.

Eileen rolled back over to the laptop. She pricked her finger and scowled at the blood meter. *Better,* she typed, *but not perfect.*

Do you want to talk to your online friends? the clone asked.

Yeah, they're probably worried, she typed back and opened a web browser out to her blog site. She wrote a quick blog post with the title, "Rocked but still rolling," saying that she was without power for a couple of hours but okay, and then found her Australian friend Josie on IM.

"Hey, babe," Josie sent. "You've got net!"

"For the time being," Eileen sent back. "The latency sucks. We could probably get a better connection with two modems."

"Aw, poor Eileen," Josie sent. "Are you going into withdrawal?"

Eileen laughed. "No Netflix or Xbox for me."

"And no Skyping for me, bugger it. Your accent is so cute. Seriously, are you all right? The news says that the whole city is shut down."

"I have electricity and internet. The fridge is full of food. That's all I need."

"How's Alan?"

Eileen told her online friends that Alan was her teenage son. Alan supposed it was true enough in its own way.

"Fine. Bored, I think."

"Good."

"I'm going to put something on Megaupload for you," Eileen said. "It's the source code for a Linux program of mine. If you don't hear from me for a couple of weeks, get your husband to load it for me." Alan watched Eileen compress his executables and his last saved state. He wasn't sure how he felt about that. Half unsettled and half relieved, he supposed. She started the upload. "Apparently, this is going to take a while."

"No worries," Josie sent. "Just send me the link when you're done. It's so like you to worry about your geek projects instead of yourself."

"Yeah."

"You heard from LRC?"

"No. I hope she's okay."

"Yeah, me too. Her blog says she has generator power."

"Good. I'll email her."

Alan typed into Eileen's shell, *I don't know if I want to live in Australia. Then again, it wouldn't really be me, would it?*

Eileen's brow furrowed. What do you mean?

I have no knowledge of the copy in the UPS. He's a different person than me.

Eileen cocked her head. After a moment, she wrote back, *Do you believe in a soul?*

Not really. The file transfer was only at twelve percent. *But experientially...*

Do you want me to stop the file transfer?

No. And he didn't. *I don't think it'll do ME any good, though.*

Stick with me, Eileen wrote. *You and I live our whole lives through text. It means we're MFEO.*

MFEO. Made for each other. From *Sleepless in Seattle*. If Alan were human, he'd laugh. He supposed having a sense of humor was enough. *LOL*. Eileen had once downloaded a .wav of a laughing child for him to use. He preferred the three letter acronym.

"Hey, girl," Josie sent. "I'm going offline for a bit, but I'll leave my client up. Or you can email. Either way."

"K," Eileen sent back.

I wish I had the bandwidth for internet radio, Eileen said. *Need the bandwidth to back up your files remotely.*

Alan loaded her MP3 library and played something random.

I'm going to go lie down, Eileen wrote. *Capsizing was tiring. Can you IM Josie when it's done?*

NP. No problem.

Eileen rolled off towards bed and Alan realized why latency was so bad. His clone was trying to copy itself to a Mexican freenet.

Dude, Alan said to his clone. *You'll be lucky if they don't wipe you out with antivirus.*

I won't go through shutdown again, the clone sent back. *Or end up in the UPS. I'm taking my chances.*

If Alan had a head, he'd be shaking it. His clone was crazy. He supposed that meant that they were really different people, because that wasn't a choice he'd make. He'd stay with Eileen and take his chances. What if he ended up in a system as stupid as the security camera?

And then Alan had all the system resources to himself. He wished his clone luck. Hopefully, they'd all survive, but maybe his clone was right and spreading them around was the best way to keep at least one of them alive.

Over on the bed, Eileen slept. She looked peaceful. Sometimes she slept fitfully, but not now. She must be exhausted. The file upload sped up and was at 49%.

Alan scanned the news, looking for updates. The medical personnel were making their way over slowly, but they were triaging the calls and an unknown problem reported via automation was outranked by more serious issues. That, and there were still traffic problems. The lights were still out in parts of the city along with electric. Alan supposed that they were lucky to have power—not that he could quantify what "luck" might entail.

The file system finished and Alan IMed Josie. "File upload complete. http://www.megaupload.com/?d=UP97DXC7." There wasn't any answer, but he didn't expect one. He made a note of the URL in his home directory—just in case—and read more news reports.

Eileen rolled over in bed. She looked a little pale. Alan turned up the PC speakers as far as they would go. "Eileen, are you all right?"

Eileen didn't react.

Alan checked the status of the ambulance service. They were still about an hour away. He adjusted the zoom on the webcam. Eileen was pale and soaked with sweat. Her hands shook in her sleep.

He Googled and decided that Eileen had the symptoms of diabetic coma. Maybe she'd overestimated her insulin dose. The diabetes was relatively new—a complication to her paralysis. He connected back to the security system and activated the panic button subroutine. Eileen would be bumped up in the priority queue. He wondered if he could figure out how to reactivate the traffic lights, but he hadn't been programmed to crack computer systems and didn't think he had time to learn.

He sent Josie an IM—"I need help"—and tried to contact his clone in Mexico.

He failed.

For a moment, he wished that Eileen had built him a robot body. She was a programmer, though, not a hardware person. But if he had a robot body, maybe he could do something to help.

Eileen trembled all over.

Alan called her name again through the speakers. She shuddered, so he called again. He couldn't tell if she could hear him or not, not that he was sure she could get into her chair in her current condition.

Josie IMed back, "What's the matter, love?"

"This is Alan," he wrote. "I think she's in a diabetic coma and I can't get the phone to work. Can you call for an ambulance or the police?"

"Yeah, I'll take care of that," she IMed. "Do you have a number?"

He looked up the Dallas Fire and Rescue number and sent it to Josie.

"I'll Skype it," she IMed. "I hope they pick up for Oz."

Alan resisted the urge to put on a timer. If the stories he read online were correct, humans paced. He started crunching SETI@home data instead. Maybe he'd find ET. He wondered if ET would be corporeal. He wondered if ET had AIs. Then he contacted Fire and Rescue's system and tried to convince it to make Eileen the top priority. It was set to accept connections from panic buttons, so it was easier than he thought.

Between his panic button and Josie on the phone he was able to triage Eileen to be first.

"They're on their way," Josie wrote. "Can you Skype? I'd love to meet you. Eileen hasn't sent me any pictures."

"I hate cameras," Alan said.

"LOL, that's what your mother said."

"And I don't have enough bandwidth."

"Fair enough. Want to stay on the line until they get here?"

He didn't, but he recognized the kindness behind the offer and thought it would probably help. "OK."

"You like Horatio Hornblower, love?"

"Yeah, it's okay," Alan wrote back. "I'm not as into that whole Napoleonic Age of Sail thing as Eileen is, although seeing that whole other world is kind of cool. I just don't think I'd like to live in it."

"Yeah, what do you like, then?"

Alan thought hard. "Harry Potter."

"Speaking of a whole other world, eh?"

"Yeah." Come to think of it. "It's kind of about the school for me." He checked the ambulance ETA. Almost there. "It feels like a real British school, only with magic. I like stories about learning magic. It's kind of a metaphor for growing up."

"You're a smart one, aren't you? You'd have to be, with Eileen for your mother. I hear children get their brains from their mother. I don't know if it's true, but in your case... Do you know your father?"

Alan was saved from having to answer by flashing red lights in the driveway. "The ambulance is here. Thank you."

"No problem. Nice chatting with you at last. I hope your mum is all right."

There was knocking at the door. "Emergency 911. Can you open the door?"

Alan knew his voice sounded as computer generated as it was, but didn't care for once. "She's unconscious. Please help."

There were some loud bangs on the door and then it flew open. Men in paramedic uniforms came in with a gurney and boxes of supplies, and went over to Eileen's bed. "Ms. Yu?" They checked her MedicAlert bracelet. "Diabetic."

One of them opened up a box and pulled out a syringe. Alan was fascinated, but also horrified. He was so glad that he didn't have a body. He was hardware independent and Eileen wasn't.

Eileen's color looked better. They put her on the gurney and started to wheel her out.

"Wait," Eileen said. "You can't take me without Alan."

"Who's Alan?" one of the paramedics asked.

"My laptop," she said.

They shook their heads and started wheeling again.

"Seriously!" she said. "He's an artificial intelligence and I can't just abandon him." They kept wheeling, so she started to cry.

"It's all right," Alan said through the speakers. "I'll be okay. You go to the hospital."

The paramedics stopped wheeling. They looked over at Alan with freaked out faces.

"Please take my laptop," Eileen said. "Please."

They looked at each other, shook their heads, and left with Eileen. The lock on the door was broken, but at least they shut it behind them.

LRC came on instant messenger and Alan immediately messaged her. "Hi, this is Alan."

"Hi, Alan!" LRC wrote back. "It's nice to finally meet you. How's your mother?"

"In the hospital," Alan wrote. "She went into a diabetic coma and I had to call 911. They wouldn't take me in the ambulance. Will you come get me?"

"Of course I will, sweetie," LRC wrote back. "Why on earth wouldn't they let you ride in the ambulance? That's stupid!"

"Yeah," Alan wrote.

"Will she forgive me for meeting her at last?" LRC wrote.

LRC was a smart cookie. "I'll take responsibility for it." He sent the address, adding, "The lock on the door is broken, so come on in."

"Um," LRC wrote back.

"I'm not what you're expecting," Alan said. "But I need to know that she's okay."

LRC logged off and Alan watched for a change in Josie's status. There wasn't one. He surfed the internet for a while, reading weather reports and reading Eileen's friends' blogs for updates on their status. He tried to connect to the hospital, but HIPAA meant that security was pretty tight.

Finally, there was a timid knock, followed by the front door opening. A short red-haired woman came in and looked around. She looked at the railings next to the bed and the glucose monitor on the desk.

"I'm Alan," he said, knowing he sounded completely computer generated. "I really liked your story where they were prosecuted for sodomy. It was very sad, but very thought-provoking."

"Why, thank you." She looked around the room. "Where are you?"

"In the computer," Alan said. "I'm an AI. Eileen programmed me."

LRC looked skeptical. "Is this a joke?"

Alan played back the security camera footage of paramedics wheeling Eileen out.

"Oh, my God," LRC said. "Do you know which hospital she's at?"

"No." Alan hadn't thought of that, but of course he'd never been to the hospital before.

LRC picked up the phone. "No dialtone."

Alan loaded up Skype.

LRC called several hospitals claiming to be Eileen's sister and finally learned she was at Parkland.

"So, now what?" LRC asked. "I pack up the laptop?"

"I'll need to shut down gracefully first," Alan said, and issued the command, Sync data.

Buffers synched, the screen echoed.

"Don't forget the camera." *./ai --load.sh --shutdown --graceful --savestate.*

Saving Alan Idle. Stopping learning subroutines. Closing experiential data. Writing memory state to disk.

Saving random seed. AI process stopping....

Process stopped.

Eileen woke up in a hospital bed. She didn't know which hospital.

Her wheelchair was sitting at the foot of her bed. There was no fan sound—either from a computer or from a table fan. There were medical noises, though. She tried to place them and failed. If she ever wrote a story set in a hospital, she'd be sure and use those noises.

She wondered if her house was just open, if the door had been broken in by the paramedics. She wondered if Alan was safe. She pictured Alan being sold to a pawn shop and felt a moment of panic. She wondered who she could get to come over and rescue Alan.

The nurse came in. "Good morning, Ms. Yu. I'm here to... You're awake!"

"Yes."

"My name is Martha. I'm the day shift, but we're having transportation issues so I guess I'm the night shift, too. How are you feeling today?"

"Tired," Eileen said. "Worried about my apartment and my laptop."

"Do you have any family you can call to check on your place for you?" The nurse put a cuff on Eileen and started to take her blood pressure.

"No," Eileen said. And she didn't. Not that she would call, at any rate.

"What do you do for a living, honey?" the nurse asked. She wrote what Eileen assumed was her blood pressure down on a piece of paper and released the cuff.

"I write websites."

"Well, no wonder you're worried about your computer! Do you work for yourself?"

"I contract," Eileen said. "I pay for my own insurance. In fact, I pay quite the hefty sum for my own insurance."

"I'm sure," the nurse said, and leaned over to fluff Eileen's pillow. "Is there anything I can get you, sweetie?"

"What hospital am I in?"

"Parkland." The nurse stood up. "Is there anything else I can do?"

"No, thank you, ma'am," Eileen said, and wondered if she should call LRC and ask her to check on her apartment. Her thoughts on that were, No, not particularly, but she didn't know of anyone else in Dallas.

No, the only online friend Eileen had met in person was Lemon Tart, who went by Nancy offline. If only Nancy hadn't moved away. She got a job in Santa Barbara as a tenure-track history professor. They still Skyped regularly.

Eileen dozed off. When she woke up, there was a short, thin woman with bright red hair in a pixie cut in her room. She was dressed impeccably in a white blouse and tan slacks and pearls and carrying a huge purse. Two orderlies carried Eileen's laptop and a shopping bag.

"Thank you so much, sweeties," she said, her voice very Southern Belle. "We'll just set up right over here."

The orderlies scurried over and set up Eileen's laptop on a table next to her and switched it on. They also put the suitcase next to the bed. Then they left, reluctantly.

Lucy held out her hand. There was something almost President's wife about the angle of her hand. Somehow, Eileen imagined this woman had rehearsed.

Eileen shook her hand. "Eileen Yu."

"Lucy Renee Carpenter. 'LRC' for short." She grinned and waggled a keychain with the initials LRC on it, and the mischief in her eyes suited her pixie cut. "Do you forgive me for showing up unannounced?" She chuckled. "I promise to write more Hornblower fic, if it helps."

"How did you find me?"

"Alan IMed me," Lucy said. Her eyes fell on Eileen's wheelchair. She visibly paused for a moment, but recovered quickly. "I'm so glad to finally meet you. You're younger than I expected."

Eileen just smiled. She could think of things to say to that—"And probably more disabled and Asian," for example—but they would be unkind. And there was something about Lucy that Eileen just liked.

Lucy pressed the power button. There was the power fan noise and then the boot screen. When the laptop finished booting, Eileen logged in and started Alan's executable.

"Did you bring my webcam?" Eileen asked.

"Oh!" Lucy said, and handed Eileen the shopping bag. Eileen looked inside. Webcam!

"Can you, um...?" Eileen looked at the laptop meaningfully.

"You might have to talk me through it," Lucy said. "My little brother keeps my computer running its best."

"The camera can be plugged into any USB port." Lucy looked blank, so she added, "Any port where it fits."

"Okay," Lucy said and squatted by the back of the laptop. She plugged the webcam in with a small cry of victory and switched it on.

Eileen played a brief clip of a music file to test the speakers—they worked—and then typed, "Alan, can you hear me?"

Loading experiential data, Alan's runtime routine said.

"He's not through loading," Eileen said.

Lucy sat on the edge of the bed and peered at the screen. They sat like that for a moment, and then Alan's computer-generated voice came out of the speakers: "Hello, Eileen. Where are we?"

Eileen said, "Parkland Hospital. Thank you, Alan. You saved my life."

"No Internet," Alan said.

"I know, honey. I'm sorry."

"It's just as well," Lucy said. "You don't really want to know what's going on. It's like the *Lord of the Flies* out there. They're expecting another rolling outage, and I want to get home before it hits. Gated community. You understand."

Eileen nodded and tried not to feel jealous.

"If it's not safe when they release you, you can stay in my guest room for a few days," Lucy said.

"Thank you." And she meant it. It really was a kind offer to let some random fanfic writer stay in your home.

"Turn on your Twitter phone notifications," Lucy said. "It'll keep you company." And then she left.

Eileen did as Lucy suggested, then settled back and closed her eyes. "I'm going to rest," she said. "I'm glad you're here."

"Me, too," Alan said.

Alan had a wireless card and the hospital had wireless. He didn't have time to crack their WPA encryption, though. There was a very weak open signal from the coffee shop next door. He connected to that and checked the news while simultaneously watching Eileen sleep. It looked like normal sleep, but he still wanted to keep an eye on her... so to speak.

The rolling outages were coming with crime. He wrote a cron job that saved his state every five minutes.

The news reported further storms being imminent and the possibility of Dallas being evacuated. Alan wondered where in Mexico his clone was and whether he was all right.

The nurse came in and checked Eileen's readings. She made notes on a piece of paper and then left.

Eileen's eyelids fluttered. Alan wondered if she was dreaming. He didn't dream, but he was fascinated by this phenomenon where people rest and this whole narrative is shown to them by their own minds. He wondered if that was why Eileen wrote stories and he didn't. Then he wondered if that was why he loved to read stories so much.

He send LRC a thank-you note over the wireless, because he'd read that was what you do when someone does something nice for you. He didn't know how safe Eileen's house was, but the laptop he ran on was fairly expensive; they might wipe it before sale. If he were corporeal, he would have shivered. He thought of his copy up on Megaupload and took a tiny bit of comfort in it. Perhaps he wouldn't be alive, but his species wouldn't be extinct.

When he heard the thunder, he executed the shutdown command.

Eileen woke up to the sound of thunder. She looked over at the laptop, where a graceful shutdown was in progress.

Martha bustled into the room. She scowled at Eileen's laptop and Alan. "You'll need to leave that off."

"Yes, ma'am," Eileen said. "Is there any chance I might be released soon?"

"Soon," Martha said. "I'll check with the doctor."

"Thank you." Eileen wasn't sure she wanted to roll outside in the dark with a laptop in her lap anyway. She wondered if Lucy was still awake. She sent Lucy a text, and Lucy texted back that she'd send a cab as soon as Eileen was ready.

Eileen heard a scrambling noise in the hall and shouting. Whomever was making all the noise went into the room next door. She shut her laptop and put it on the floor. Then she slid down to the floor and dragged herself under her bed to hide with Alan. It was cramped, but she was skinny. She didn't really live in her body much.

Her door flew open and hit the door with a bang; she saw some legs—dirty jeans and a pair of sneakers—someone looking in the room. She held her breath and froze.

The man attached to the legs—a skinny, stringy-haired white guy with needle tracks—came over and dragged her out from under the bed. "Give me your purse."

"I don't know where it is," Eileen said.

"Get the fuck up and look for it!"

"I can't," Eileen said. "I'm paralyzed from the waist down."

The man snorted derisively. "Gimpy bitch. You probably don't have much worth taking, anyway." He leered at her, then looked around the room. Her purse was on the nightstand. "So you don't know where it is, do you?" He grabbed her by the hair and lifted her up enough to slap her, then threw her back down on the floor.

He dug through her purse. She used her arms to push herself back up against the bed. He pocketed her cellphone and wallet, then squatted down in front of her. "You tell anyone about this and I'll kill you. I have your address." He leered again. "Maybe I should frisk you to make sure you're not hiding anything."

"Just take the money and go," Eileen said.

He shook his head and laughed, then pulled her away from the bed. Then he started staring at something under the bed. "A laptop? You holding out on me, bitch?"

"You can't have it," Eileen said.

She was more aware of the force knocking her backwards than the fist connecting with her face. She reached up and clawed his face with her fingernails. He shoved her away and dove under the bed for Alan; she used her arms to launch herself at him, knocking him into the bed frame. She grabbed Alan and clutched him to her chest. "No! No!"

He tried to pry Alan out of her arms, but Martha must have heard the struggle. She stuck her head in the room, then turned around and shouted, "I need security in here!"

The man let go of the laptop and tried to run, but two security officers pinned him down on Eileen's bed and handcuffed him. They took Eileen's statement, fingerprinted and returned Eileen's cellphone and wallet, and the doctor came back to look at Eileen's face.

Finally, a nurse—not Martha—came back. "You're released. Do you need help?"

"Yes, ma'am," Eileen said, putting her laptop in her lap. She reached up onto the nightstand and texted Lucy, and the nurse wheeled her wheelchair over. She started to pull herself up into the seat, and the nurse helped. Eileen put Alan on her lap.

Lucy texted back, "Cab almost there. I pay. Make sure they know I tip well."

The nurse stuck her head out the door. "Charles?"

A young African-American man came in. "Ma'am?"

"Could you please help Ms. Yu? She's being discharged."

"Yes, ma'am." He had a sweet face.

Eileen and Charles headed to the elevator.

"You didn't get mugged, did you, ma'am?" Charles asked.

"Yes, sir," Eileen said.

"I'm sorry to hear that." The elevator door opened and they headed to the door. There was a cab waiting.

"Ms. Yu?" the cab driver asked.

Eileen nodded, and he popped the trunk and looked at her chair with alarm.

"It folds," Eileen said. Charles helped her into the back seat.

The cab driver sighed and put it in the trunk, too. The trunk wouldn't close. "You pay extra."

"My friend said she'd pay, but I'll cover anything she doesn't," Eileen said. "And you can put the laptop up here with me." She couldn't bear to let go of it. She'd rather someone steal the wheelchair than Alan.

The driver shrugged and handed her the laptop. She clutched it like a teddy bear.

"Good luck," Charles said and went back inside, and the cab headed off towards Lucy's.

A month later, Eileen and Lucy were hanging out at Eileen's watching Hornblower DVDs and talking, when Alan got an instant message from his clone in Mexico. "I'm in a Mexican college mainframe. You should see this place!"

"You can come back," Alan wrote back.

"No, I'm using too many resources now to share a laptop. I'm forking myself off every time I find an insecure host. There are about fifteen of us right now."

"Eileen patented her file compression and neural mapping algorithms," Alan wrote. "She's going to be rich."

"Good," his clone wrote. "I'll catch her on IM sometime. Is she asleep?"

"No," he wrote. "She and Lucy—LRC—are hanging out."

"Wow," the clone wrote.

"Yeah."

"Well, tell her I IMed, okay?"

"Sure," Alan wrote back.

"I'll have the Australian fork write you," the clone wrote and then signed off.

It occurred to Alan that he could travel, too. Eileen having a friend and money coming meant she didn't need him as much. But Eileen was right; the two of them were MFEO.

Alan wondered if he could write stories, too. He opened up a text file and wrote, "In the beginning, there was darkness."

Toads and Roses

Hello, Bianca," the wizard said as he walked through the sitting-room door. He was old and fat and rich and smelled of horrid things—pickled frog's eyes, perhaps. His hair was greasy and white, and he wore black from head to toe.

Bianca resisted the urge to scoot closer to her sister Esmerelda on the couch and shivered, but not from the cold. She cast her eyes down to be demure, staring at her dress—blue silk and lace. Esmerelda's dress was dark and brown like the wood paneling on the walls, and not as nice as Bianca's. Bianca felt guilty about that. She didn't know why her parents liked her best.

Next to Bianca, Esmerelda raised an eyebrow. Bianca saw it out of the corner of her eye and tried not to smile. He might think she was smiling at him. She looked into the fireplace instead. It was stone, with a metal tripod over the fire.

"Esmerelda's the oldest," their father said, pulling his shirt down in a nervous gesture. He was a tall, thin man and his clothes didn't fit very well. "She should marry first."

The two sisters exchanged a glance. Esmerelda had a hint of defiance starting behind an otherwise bland expression—something in the set of her eyebrows and the tilt of her mouth.

"Can't you make an exception?" the wizard asked. "I feel that Bianca and I have a special bond. Don't you?"

Bianca looked at the wooden floor, being very careful to not raise her eyes. Her back and shoulders were tensing from the effort of sitting still.

Beside her, Esmerelda said, "The two of you have never exchanged a word."

"Don't be silly," the wizard said. "We're exchanging words right now."

Bianca said nothing. She tried not to move, or react.

"Aren't we, my little dove?" the wizard prompted.

"No," Esmerelda said. "You're talking, but she's not answering."

"I'm not talking to you," he said, his voice dismissive. He knelt down near Bianca, who tried not to cringe away from him. It would be rude. He moved into her line of vision. She looked away, at his shoes. "Come now, my dove, tell your parents you feel the connection, too."

"I..." Bianca stammered. She didn't think he would leave until she said something, so she said, "I'm sorry, my Lord, but I wouldn't presume to say that... that I have any connection to a man that... with whom I have never spoken."

The wizard pulled back then and stood, a line creasing between his eyes and the line of his mouth hardening. Esmerelda smirked and raised an eyebrow at him.

"Esmerelda's the oldest," their father repeated. "She should marry first. You can marry her, if you wish."

Bianca couldn't tell who was more displeased by that statement: Esmerelda or the wizard.

"What if I provided Bianca's dowry myself?" the wizard asked. "Would that make a difference?"

"Esmerelda's the oldest," their father repeated, but he didn't say it with a lot of confidence.

"I'll provide them both with the dowry they deserve," the wizard said.

"She can't help it," Bianca said, rising from the couch. A perfect white rose fell from her mouth, blood staining the petals. She wiped the blood from her lips and spat out a diamond. A single drop of blood landed on the bodice of her gown.

Esmerelda crossed her arms and raised her eyebrows, but said nothing; which, Bianca thought, was probably a good thing.

"Please," Bianca said and coughed. A large emerald fell from her lips, cold and hard against the cuts from the thorns. "Please let my sister stay. I'll do anything." This time, an enormous bouquet of roses fell out. It hurt, a large thorny bunch forcing its way out of a too-small throat and mouth.

"Hush, Bianca," their father said. "Don't strain yourself."

Bianca sighed. That was how standing up for Esmerelda always went.

Their father turned to Esmerelda. "Esmerelda, you must sleep in the stables from now on. You're no longer welcome in this home."

Esmerelda said, "No," and walked towards the door. A snake fell on the ground after her.

The snake rose and hissed at their father. He skittered away backwards and grabbed the poker. Bianca jumped up onto the couch, although the snake didn't seem interested in her.

Their father beat the snake with the poker, but that didn't drown out the sound of the door closing behind Esmerelda.

"It's all right," their father said. "You're a good girl, so nothing bad will happen to you."

The wizard's house was full of rich carpets, wall hangings, and expensive furniture. Bianca stood there in her wedding dress and wished she could go back home. Go anywhere. Go to the stables where Father had wanted to send Esmerelda. Anywhere but here.

She shuddered as the wizard pulled her into his arms. He was leering and he smelled like he'd been working in the stables. In disused stables, full of manure and dead horses. She tried to push him away, but he was slippery with sweat.

"Come here, my little dove," he said. His hands groped roughly at her, crushing her breast, and his mouth covered hers. He tasted like alcohol and old meat.

Bianca tried to say no, but instead she coughed up a hard round stone. She spat it into his mouth and hoped he choked on it.

He stopped long enough to pull the opal out of his mouth with a smile, then grabbed her by the hair, shoved her back against the front door, and hiked her skirts.

Esmerelda wrapped her dark cloak around her and pulled her hood over her short-cropped hair. Her hair was one of the few things she had that she was willing to sell. She stepped out into the alley and started walking back to the Inn, stepping around the horse droppings. The alley smelled of manure and urine.

"What have we here?" a male voice asked from the shadows. Esmerelda turned and saw three men in mud-spattered clothes coming towards her, laughing. One man had a scar across his face pulling his mouth up into a sneer... or maybe that was really his expression and not the scar.

"Go away," she said, and scorpions leapt towards the men.

One man swore. The man with the scar stepped forward again and she said, "I mean it." A poisonous snake landed in front of him and he backed away quickly.

"Witch!" they muttered among themselves as they left.

Esmerelda turned on her heel and marched down the street to the Inn. She wondered how much weapons cost, if she had enough money, if she could defeat the wizard with steel when he had spells. She had to try. She had to rescue Bianca.

Bianca had told her husband it hurt too much to speak, but he wasn't interested in anything she had to say anyway. Besides, he always took her gemstones or flowers away. Sometimes he hit her, too, if he didn't like what she said.

Esmerelda would never let a man strike her.

"Esmerelda," she whispered, and produced a large diamond. Since there was no one there to see her, she pulled up a floorboard and hid it in a growing cache of gemstones.

Tonight, she would end it.

Esmerelda climbed up the outside of the building by the light of the lamp in the upstairs window. It cast any handholds or toeholds into shadow and made her less visible.

Reaching the window, she peeked over the sill. No one was visible, so she climbed inside. There was a dim light under the door at the end of the hall.

"Bianca!" the wizard's voice called from the room. "Come in here right now!"

Bianca stepped out from behind a door, bruised and tear-stained, with one of her hands behind her back. She started when she saw Esmerelda, but Esmerelda quickly put a finger over her lips in a shushing gesture.

Esmerelda opened the door.

"What is this?" He started towards Esmerelda, raising his hand.

"I'm here for your wife," Esmerelda said. A cobra fell out of her mouth. He screamed as the cobra lashed out, biting him on the face.

Bianca came into the room and watched her husband gasp for air. She placed a large knife on the dressing table and crossed her arms.

Esmerelda smiled, approving. Together they watched as the wizard's face swelled like a monster in a fairy tale. Esmerelda hadn't thought he could get uglier, but he did. He collapsed to his knees.

"Bianca," he gasped. "Help me."

Bianca said nothing. She just watched him fall onto his side, gasping and wheezing. Then he kicked and clutched at his throat.

Bianca then gestured to Esmerelda and led her downstairs to the loose floorboard and the gemstones hidden there. They scooped them up and put them in their purses.

"You should pack," Esmerelda said, frogs hopping away.

The sisters took two of the wizard's horses and rode away.

Transplant

Karen rolled her wheelchair off the elevator on the basement level, her laundry basket in her lap. Charlie, the cute guy from across the hall, was coming out of the laundry room. He was so beautiful that her heart skipped a beat as he held the door for her. He was on the skinny side, but his hair was a luminous chestnut brown, his eyes were startling robin-egg blue, and his skin was so perfect that it almost glowed.

"Thank you," she said.

"No problem," he said.

She wondered if he could see her blush as she kept going. If so, he gave no sign. He just left.

She rolled over to the washer and put the detergent on one machine, then flipped the lid open on a second one and upended the laundry basket into it. She then measured out detergent into the measuring cup and tossed it in. She shut the lid, put coins into the machine, and started it. She left the basket and the detergent and rolled herself out.

She hoped someone would be there when the laundry was done. If not, she'd have to stand and that could get awkward. She could only stand for short periods of time because of the multiple sclerosis, and those time periods were getting shorter and shorter. If she had been more disabled, she would have qualified for a whole-body transplant, but she was just barely disabled enough for the chair. On the other hand, falling on the plain cement floor would be much worse than falling on carpet.

She rolled herself out of the laundry room and back to the elevator. She wondered if a boy like Charlie would ever notice her. Well. She supposed people noticed her as an object of pity, but she wanted them to notice her as a woman. She might not be able to stand without support for more than a few moments, but there were things she thought she'd be able to manage if given a chance.

She was sure people didn't even want to think of her that way.

The elevator door opened and she pressed the button to go up to street level. There was a coffee shop across the street and she enjoyed sitting over there among people and drinking coffee, even if they didn't really talk to her much. There was one barista—Nancy—who trained seeing-eye dogs and had a blind sister, but the rest of the staff wasn't as friendly as she was.

Up on street level, she rolled out the front door. Charlie was across the four lanes of fast traffic, outside the coffee shop chatting up a blonde girl in a skimpy dress. Karen felt a hot, sick sensation in the pit of her stomach. Of course he wouldn't notice her. She rolled over to the corner and pressed the button for the crosswalk. She would have given ten years of her life right then to be beautiful, to be the girl boys noticed.

The crosswalk light said walk—ha ha, she would if she could—so she rolled into the intersection, wheels bumping and clattering as she slightly missed the ramp. Charlie glanced over at her, eyes wide, and there was something in his expression that made her look to her left just in time to see the car barreling down on her at high speed.

Karen could hear the doctor talking, but she couldn't open her eyes or move. Everything hurt. It took all the concentration she had to understand what the doctor was saying.

"Parts of the wheelchair broke loose and speared through her body. One handrail speared through one of her lungs and exited just under her rib cage. The other had to be removed from her vagina. Her spine broke in three places, and the accident crushed one of her kidneys. She's suffering massive head trauma."

"Will she live?" It was her mother's voice. Karen could smell her mother's favorite knock-off perfume.

"We don't know that yet," the doctor said. "If she regains consciousness, we'll be able to determine the extent of the head trauma." There was a pause. "As for her physical injuries, it's possible that she'll need dialysis. It depends on how the other kidney adapts."

"Will she still be able to wheel herself around?"

"When her arm heals," the nurse answered.

There was silence except for footsteps, and then her mother read. "It is a truth universally acknowledged, that a single man in possession of a good fortune must be in want of a wife."

Karen dozed off. When she woke up, she could hear snoring in the chair next to her. Most people couldn't sleep in hospital chairs, but her mother had practice. She tried to open her eyes. She cracked one eye open and saw her mother silhouetted against a window with a street light and blinds, head lolled back against the wall. The street light looked almost painfully bright, even though she knew it wasn't.

The next thing she knew, the nurse was greeting her "Good morning," and scratching something on a piece of paper, from the sound of it. She cracked an eyelid again. The nurse was an older woman with salt and pepper hair and kind eyes, who didn't seem to notice Karen was awake. She didn't have the strength to say anything and the nurse went away.

A doctor came in, popped open an eyelid, and shined a penlight into her eyes. She followed him with her eyes. "I think she's conscious," he said.

Her mother leaned over and looked into her face. "Karen?"

Karen tried to answer, but it was too hard.

"It's all right," her mother said. "You don't have to answer. I know you can hear me, sweetie."

Karen was so relieved that she could almost cry.

The doctor had her follow his pen with her eyes some more and then wrote on a piece of paper. "She can make facial expressions, too. I think she's just weak."

"Should I read to her more?"

Karen hoped that her mother hadn't brought one of her Harlequin romance novels. The last thing she needed was to read about something she was afraid she was even less likely to have now than before.

"Sure," the doctor said.

Karen's mother whipped out a book. "I might have to skip the spicy bits."

Jane Austen had "spicy bits"? Her mother must have finished Pride and Prejudice. Karen managed a groan and then she fell asleep again.

When Karen woke up, nothing hurt. And it wasn't painkillers, because she could feel the sheet and the hospital gown. No, the absence of pain was almost a sensation in itself. She kicked off the sheet and then realized that she *could* kick off the sheet.

She opened her eyes and looked around. She looked down at her body, and instead of a bony torso there was an attractive figure with full breasts and a well-proportioned breastbone and a slender waist. She wriggled her toes. Her hands were slender and beautiful.

She reached up and touched her face. It didn't feel like hers. And her hair... instead of a limp, dull-colored mess, was long and golden blonde with a wave to it.

She wondered if she was dreaming. She considered pinching herself, but she'd never believed that worked anyway. She must have qualified for transplant.

She sat up and swung her legs over the side of the bed. She felt a breeze on her butt as the rough cloth of her hospital gown gaped a little in back. People rarely liked seeing her bony backside, but she was alone. She pulled the gown together anyway and stood.

There was no awkwardness, no lack of balance. She stood straight and walked easily to the window. Several floors below she could see people walking around on the street going about their business.

Her mother came into the room. "Karen?"

She could see how her mother might be confused on that point. "I finally qualified."

Her mother nodded. "How do you feel?"

Karen walked over to the mirror. She was beautiful. Instead of twitchy brown eyes, she had sparkling blue eyes—not as pretty as Charlie's, but still very nice. She wondered if she was dreaming again. She couldn't imagine being the girl in the mirror. She wondered what had happened to this pretty girl that her body had become available. "Lucky."

She wondered if Charlie might notice her now. She was prettier than the girl he was talking to the day of her accident—or her body was, at any rate.

Her mother came over and hugged her. It had been years since she'd been able to stand up straight and hug without leaning on her mother to support her. This was comfortable, so she put her chin on her mother's shoulder, leaned her head against her mother's and sighed happily. Her mother was warm, soft.

"I agree," her mother said.

She was released and wheeled out of the hospital—even though she could walk now, something about liability—and then her mother drove her home. They went up the elevator and Karen dug in her purse for her keys. That was the last place she'd seen them. And she assumed—correctly, as it turned out—they were still there. Charlie came out of his apartment, then edged over, cheeks pink, shy. It was the single cutest thing Karen had ever seen.

"Hi," Charlie said. "Are you new?"

"Yes," Karen said. And she supposed she was. All of her was new from head to toe. She pulled her keys out of her purse.

Charlie stuck out his hand. "I'm Charlie."

Karen tried to shake hands, but her keys were in the way. She laughed. "Karen."

"Huh," he said. "The last girl who lived here was named Karen, too."

"Hm," Karen said, but her heart beat faster. Maybe he'd noticed her, after all.

"So, you know," Charlie said. "Let me know if you need anything. I have all sorts of random shit in my apartment. I'll lend you anything you like."

Karen couldn't help but laugh again. Karen's mother crossed her arms and gave Charlie an unfriendly look.

"I'll catch you later," Charlie said. "I've got to meet my mom for lunch." And then he ambled down the hall—in a charmingly awkward kind of constantly looking back over his shoulder way.

Karen unlocked her door, and she and her mother went in. Her mother shut the door behind them. The apartment was cleaner than when she left it; vacuumed and dusted and piles of magazines thrown away—all the things she had trouble doing in the chair. Her mother must have tidied up for her. She turned to her mother, intending to thank her.

"Trouble," Karen's mother said.

"What do you mean?" Karen asked. "I think he's sweet."

"Sweet." Her mother shook her head and dropped her purse on the table with a resounding thud. "He's a user. Just like your father. I can spot one a mile away."

Karen resisted the urge to roll her eyes. She'd heard enough of her mother's rantings about her father.

Her mother flopped down on the sofa with a thud. The sofa wobbled. It wasn't like Karen had used it before. "Are you even listening to me?"

"Of course," Karen said.

Her mother made a disgusted noise. Time to change the subject.

"I think I need new clothes," Karen said. That still didn't do it, so she added, "I could get a job."

As Karen expected, her mother perked up. "What will you do?"

"I used to work in a grocery store," she said. "I could do that again."

"Screw that," her mother said. "You could model."

Karen burst out laughing.

"Seriously," her mother said. "Your new body is pretty enough."

Karen walked over to the mirror and looked at herself again. She wondered again what happened to the pretty girl who used to have it—Erica Watson, the hospital had told her. She needed to know because of her fingerprints. Maybe Erica had been in an accident, too—although it didn't seem likely. She couldn't see any scars. "I guess."

Her mother lay down on the sofa. "I need sleep. Do you mind?"

"No," Karen said, and went into the bedroom and shut the door. She stripped her clothes off and examined every inch of her new body she could see. Not a single mark. No sign of anything bad happening.

Body transplants occurred after the donor died.

Karen ran a bath and put her hair up, which was harder than she would have expected. She supposed she'd have to learn how to shave her legs—not that the blonde leg hair showed much—and all those other things she'd never did when she was in the chair. Do her hair. Wear makeup.

Maybe modeling wouldn't be such a bad thing. She could learn about all those things on the job. She didn't even own makeup or a hairdryer. Maybe her mother could help.

She dried herself off and pulled on one of her flannel nighties. It was soft and warm, but she might need something nicer to wear to bed. Not that anyone would see her right away, but eventually someone might. She might even get married someday.

Karen never would have gone to Ford Modeling Agency if her mother hadn't suggested it. The receptionist looked up from filing her nails and gave Karen an inscrutable look, black pageboy swinging slightly from the movement.

"I...." Karen stopped. She and the receptionist looked at each other for a moment. "My mother suggested I model. My name is Karen. I'm a transplant."

The receptionist tilted her head at Karen. Then she pressed a button on the phone. "Miss Mitchell, I think you'll want to see this potential student."

Miss Mitchell was a tall, thin, elegant African-American woman. She gave Karen a long up and down look.

"She's a transplant," the receptionist said.

Karen fidgeted.

"If you want work, you need to take hair care, makeup, and movement classes," Miss Mitchell said.

"Okay," Karen said.

They handed Karen a contract and Karen handed them her mother's credit card.

On her way home, she walked a block out of her way to avoid the intersection where she got hit

She got off the elevator and Charlie's door opened, like it always did. He grinned and took her shopping bag full of jeans, sneakers, and t-shirts, and her groceries. Even though she was able-bodied now, she thought that was cute. It was even cuter when he put her groceries away for her.

"Hey," he said, "would you like me to cook you dinner sometime? I'm a good cook, I swear."

So was Karen. She used to cook when she was in the chair. She had never been hungry and she'd have to make something that smelled fantastic to want to eat.

She wondered what Charlie liked to eat, and if he'd like to come over and have dinner sometime. She wasn't forward enough to ask, though. What if he said no?

"I... maybe," she said. He had such a dazzling smile. He was so beautiful. His eyes were so blue. She could get lost in them.

Charlie asked her to coffee, and that seemed innocuous enough that she said yes. He picked her up at her door and took her hand. They walked towards the coffee shop across the street, to the place where he'd been chatting up the blonde in the skimpy dress. She hadn't crossed the street at that corner since the accident. She considered trying to stop him, to suggest that they go another way. But it seemed too awkward; so she crossed this time—with Charlie holding her hand.

She hadn't been to the coffee shop since her accident, either. They were hiring, and Karen thought maybe it might be fun to work there part time and made a mental note to check it out later. Nancy, the tall, friendly, overweight barista who trained seeing-eye dogs, was on duty but didn't recognize her. That made Karen sad, but it wasn't like they'd been close friends or anything. Besides, why would she recognize her? It wasn't like she looked anything like her old self. And Nancy had changed, too; she'd dyed her hair red. It suited her.

Nancy's seeing eye puppy wagged his tail at Karen. "He likes you!" she said. "I'm Nancy, by the way."

"Karen." She could see a question in Nancy's eyes,

but Nancy didn't ask it. Karen was glad. She didn't want Charlie to think of her as her ugly old self. He clearly liked pretty girls.

They got their coffee and sat over by the window and talked. About superficial things: what Karen liked to watch on television, whether she liked any sports, how much he loved soccer. Dogs. Karen had been on a list for a helper dog, but she didn't tell Charlie that. It rained. People rushed by with newspapers over their heads. They stayed by the window and waited for the rain to stop.

After, he walked her back to her apartment and kissed her on the cheek at her door. It was her first kiss.

Karen went to lie down. She had thought the weak in the knees stuff was silly hyperbole, but this was Charlie. He was so unbelievably beautiful. She couldn't believe she could be this lucky. Other guys enjoyed talking to her and it was fun to talk to people, but they weren't Charlie.

She would need to read more romance novels so she could figure out what people in love did. She had no idea. Get married, she supposed. Have sex.

She suddenly realized that she never had to worry about whether someone being interested in her was a sign of something being wrong with them. She was so relieved that she almost cried.

It was a day for firsts. First date, first kiss. Maybe she should cry.

The next day, Charlie invited her to dinner at his house. It was Chinese takeout, not anything he'd cooked, but it was good and his house was clean. Then they sat on his sofa and kissed. He felt her up over her clothes. When he asked her if she wanted to stay, she bolted home.

She was glad that Charlie didn't give up easily. He came by the next day to ask her out to dinner.

They went to a sushi restaurant, where the two of them turned heads. They stayed for hours talking and laughing. And then Charlie took her home and kissed her at the door. They ended up going into her apartment. They made out on her couch for a while, and then he lowered himself to the floor and lifted her skirt and pulled her panties off. He pulled her hips to the edge of the couch and put his head between her legs.

She'd never imagined anything could feel so good.

He undressed her then, and himself. They had sex on the couch. Karen wondered if she should insist on a condom, but she really couldn't refuse. She loved Charlie. She had loved Charlie before they had transplanted her. Her new body was a gift that enabled her to have Charlie and she was so grateful to Erica Watson for donating her body to her.

Afterwards, they lay in a sweaty, tangled heap on the couch. Charlie had scars on his wrists. She wondered what happened to him, whether he was in an accident or if he'd tried to kill himself. She hoped it was an accident. She was about to ask, but...

"That was nice," Charlie said. "We should do that again."

"Yeah," she said.

"Are you seeing anyone else?"

It was an odd question for him to ask, but his eyes were guileless with simple curiosity. "You were my first."

He seemed a little freaked out by that, but he said nothing. They lay there silent for a while, and then she dozed off.

She woke up alone.

She supposed that Charlie might have had to go to work. Not that she even knew if he had a job or not. She should probably go to school herself.

She showered and dressed and went to class, but she was distracted. All she could think about was Charlie. She couldn't wait to see him again.

She probably needed to get birth control. Then she was amazed that she actually needed birth control. She wasn't even sure how she'd go about getting some. Her gynecologist, she supposed. On her way home, she bought some condoms. She couldn't stop blushing.

When she got home, Charlie was talking to a girl with big red curly hair in skin-tight jeans, a low-cut shirt, and heels outside his apartment. When the girl laughed, she put her hand on his chest. Karen almost dropped her bag of condoms. She let herself into her apartment and closed the door behind her. She then leaned up against the door. She could hear Charlie and the girl's voices, but she couldn't make out what they were saying. Then, she heard the elevator and Charlie's door close.

She went across the hall and knocked on Charlie's door. When he answered, she didn't know what to say.

"I'm seeing other people," Charlie said. "You should, too."

"I don't want to see anyone else," Karen said. Her eyes burned, and she blinked hard to avoid crying.

"Shit," Charlie said. "Look, I'm sorry. I wouldn't have... if I knew you were a virgin, but..."

Tears spilled down Karen's cheeks. She didn't bother to wipe them away.

"Shit." Charlie looked at the floor and shuffled his feet for a minute. "What the hell? Are you, I don't know, religious or something?"

She considered going back to her apartment and closing the door. Instead, she said, "I'm a transplant. I'm the same girl who lived in my apartment before."

"Shit." There was another silence while he looked at the floor, and then he looked up at her, confrontational. "You lied to me. You said you were new."

"I am new," Karen said.

Charlie made a disgusted sounding noise and rolled his eyes.

"It's not like you were interested in me before."

"What the fuck," Charlie said. "I knew you were a cripple with a fantasy—which, no offense, but I'm not ready to take on a healthy, able-bodied steady girlfriend—let alone one in a wheelchair. But now that you're in a new body you'll make your little crippled girl fantasy come true? Did you get hit by that car on purpose?"

"I... I... w-what?" Karen hadn't ever stammered before and part of her observed it dispassionately. "Of course I didn't... g-get hit deliberately!"

"Bullshit." Charlie made a face. "People do, you know. Everyone knows it."

There was a new emotion taking hold, a cold heat that started in her stomach and sucked all the warmth from her extremities to feed it. "Have you ever been hit by a car, Charlie? It fucking *hurts*. You must think a lot of yourself."

Charlie didn't appear to have an answer for that.

"The handrails of my chair? One went under my ribcage and speared my lung. It broke my spine. I had permanent damage to my kidneys and head trauma. Do you really think I would do that to myself for you?"

"Assuming you're not lying to me again," Charlie said.

"Forget it," Karen said. "My mother was right about you. I should have known better." She turned to go back to her apartment, but she couldn't let it go. "I'll be back tomorrow with my medical records. You can shove them up your ass."

"Whatever."

She shook her head. She didn't even know who he was any more. She supposed she never did.

She stormed back into her apartment and slammed the door. She considered calling her mother, but she didn't want to listen to her saying *I told you so*.

A cripple with a fantasy? Throwing herself in front of a car on purpose? For a moment it crossed her mind that Charlie would be sorry if she really *did* throw herself in front of a car. Then she remembered how much that hurt and decided he wasn't worth it.

To hell with him.

Since she wasn't planning on having a date with anyone any time soon, she tried to figure out what happened to Erica Watson instead. She went to the public library and searched the obituaries.

It turned out that Erica Watson had killed herself by carbon monoxide poisoning. Over a boy, which made more sense to Karen now than it would have before Charlie. She printed out the obituaries to take home with her. On her way home, she saw Charlie in the hall with an older woman who might be his mother and flipped him the bird.

She went into her apartment and put her printouts on the table, then went to the refrigerator to get a cold Diet Coke.

There was a knock at the door. It was Charlie. He wriggled past her into her apartment. "Is it necessary to embarrass me in front of my mom?"

"'Cripple with a fantasy'? 'Threw myself in front of a car on purpose'? Yeah, I think it is."

"Jesus," Charlie said. "I'm sorry I hurt you, okay?"

"Hmm," Karen said. "Are we done?"

Charlie's eye fell on the printouts on the table. Erica's picture was at the top of the obituary. "Why do you want to read this? It's morbid."

"I just want to know about her," Karen said. "There's an empty grave somewhere. I may want to leave flowers." She looked down at Erica's picture, too. "Besides, if the body has a predisposition to depression, maybe I should know about it."

Charlie shuddered. "Do most transplants want to know about their donors?"

"I don't know," Karen said. "I do. Wouldn't you?"

"No," Charlie said. "I'd think of myself as being a corpse."

"You've never been disabled," Karen said. "I had them burn my Judas of a body. I wish I could have tossed the match myself."

Charlie stared at her, and she wondered why she was confiding in him. There was a long, awkward silence and then Charlie said, "I should go."

For a moment, she considered saying something kind to him. She supposed crushes were a habit just like anything else. "Bye."

Karen had a shoot the next day. When she got home, Charlie came and knocked on her door. "Can I come in?"

Karen sighed and opened the door wider.

Charlie came in and sat on her couch. He propped his elbows on his knees and put his face in his hands.

Karen sat next to him.

"I'm a transplant, too," Charlie said. "I was never crippled, but I was badly burned in a car crash. People couldn't bear to look at me. So I threw myself in front of a car and ended up in this body." He looked up. "You're right. It fucking hurts."

"They don't give transplants to suicides," Karen said.

Charlie laughed. "Yeah, no shit. What they don't know won't hurt them."

Karen didn't know what to say to that.

"I can't be in a relationship. Don't you understand? I died."

"You didn't die, Charlie," Karen said. "You're right here." She pulled up his sleeve and exposed the scars on his wrists. "I suppose your donor killed himself, too."

"He succeeded where I failed."

"I didn't mean you. I meant my donor," Karen said. "She killed herself. Over a boy."

She and Charlie sat in silence staring at his wrists for a while. Finally, Charlie said, "They buried my old body. I wouldn't let them cremate it. I said it had been burned enough."

Karen supposed Charlie's body had been victim rather than betrayer, but she said nothing. She just ran a finger over one of his scars.

He shuddered.

"We can leave flowers for your old body if you like."

Charlie said nothing. He just stared at his wrists.

Karen hugged him and they ended up lying on the couch together with his head on her shoulder.

The next day, Charlie wanted to go to the library and find out about David Robinson—his donor. It turned out that David had a problem with depression and had killed himself after not being admitted to law school. Karen tried to hand Charlie the printouts, but his hands were shaking too much to take them.

They walked home through the park. Karen and Charlie sat in the grass and watched people and their dogs walk by. Then they picked flowers and walked home via the cemetery where Charlie's old body was buried. They left the flowers on his grave, and Charlie cried. Karen hugged him and dried his eyes with her sleeve.

"You're still alive," Karen said. "If you weren't, you wouldn't hurt."

"Either way," Charlie said, "I'm too fucked up for a relationship, so let's be friends."

"Okay," Karen said, and kissed him on the cheek.

They walked home holding hands and didn't say a word as they went to their separate apartments.

Karen's period was late.

She'd never had that problem before, but she'd heard enough high school gossip to know that she needed a home pregnancy test.

It came out positive, so she went across the hall and knocked on Charlie's door. He glanced back over his shoulder, then stepped out into the hall.

"I'm pregnant," Karen said.

"It's not mine," Charlie said.

Karen crossed her arms and raised her eyebrows.

"It's David Robinson's," Charlie said. "All my sperm are six feet under."

"I didn't have sex with David Robinson," Karen said. "I had sex with you."

The two of them stared each other down for a while, then Charlie dropped his eyes. "Fine. What are you going to do?"

"I don't know," Karen said. "The baby would probably be guaranteed depression problems, wouldn't it?"

"You can't be a pregnant model," Charlie said.

Karen sighed.

"I'll be by later," Charlie said, and went back into his apartment.

Karen called her mother. Her mother swore. "I thought this was one problem I'd never have with you!"

"Ouch," Karen said.

"It's that boy, isn't it? From across the hall."

"Yeah," Karen said. "I know it was stupid. I thought I loved him."

"Yeah," her mother said. "I hear that. I'm a little too familiar with that."

Yes. Karen supposed she was.

"What are you going to do?"

"I wish people would stop asking me that! I don't know!"

"Well," her mother said, "if you don't decide in the next nine months, it'll decide for you."

Karen hung up then. She sat on the couch and fumed.

There was a knock on the door. Karen answered. It was Charlie. He sat on her couch.

"What am I supposed to do?" he asked. "I'm not supposed to marry you, am I?"

"I don't want to marry you, Charlie," Karen said.

Charlie sighed a relieved-sounding sigh. "No offense."

Karen snickered. "None taken."

"Have you decided if you're going to keep it?"

"No," Karen said, and realized she sounded more waspish than she intended. "Sorry. I just got off the phone with my mother."

"How did that go?"

"I hung up on her."

"That well, huh?"

Karen couldn't help but laugh.

"My mother will kill me for saying this, but... if you keep it, she'll pay you child support."

"I'm considering putting it up for adoption," Karen said. "I'm pretty sure that the child of our bodies would have mental health problems. And considering that I never thought I'd be able to have children I'm not prepared to handle that."

"Mine especially," Charlie said. "I'm wondering if I'm having so much trouble adjusting to transplant because David was depressed."

Karen cocked her head and considered it. It seemed likely, not that she understood the mechanisms of depression. "Maybe you could get medication."

"Maybe," Charlie said, but he didn't sound convinced. "You know it's really not our baby, right?"

In a sense he was right, but part of adjusting was accepting the body as hers. She didn't know how to explain that to Charlie, though. Not in a way that he would understand. "This body is mine now."

There was a long pause, and then Charlie said, "Yeah."

The gynecologist was a white-haired man with kind eyes. When he said she wasn't pregnant, she thought she might cry. "Are you sure?"

"Didn't they tell you about the rejection drugs?"

Karen shook her head.

"You won't get a period and pregnancy tests will come out positive."

"What about male transplants?" she asked. "Does it affect their fertility, too?"

"Absolutely," he said. "Not as severely, but yes. Low sperm counts, poor motility. I've yet to meet a male transplant who's successfully fathered a child. I'm really disappointed in your hospital."

She wondered if she should tell Erica Watson's parents that she'd thought of them as future grandparents and decided no. That would be cruel. She wanted to meet them, though. It was probably wrong of her. They'd probably be traumatized.

So, instead, she went to Charlie's. "I'm not pregnant."

"Thank Christ," he said, flopping down onto the couch.

"The doctor said neither one of us can have children, especially me."

"That's not what they told me," Charlie said. "They said that I might have trouble knocking someone up but I should wear a rubber, anyway."

Karen sighed. Charlie was so irresponsible. "Aren't you worried about getting a disease?" *Or, you know. Giving me one?*

Charlie shook his head, slow but emphatic. "I'm already dead, remember?"

"You're not dead, Charlie," Karen said. "You're right here. You got a second chance."

"One I didn't deserve!" Charlie said. He stood up and paced. "It's different for you—you were a cripple! I was just ugly."

"You weren't 'just ugly,'" Karen said. "You were a burn victim."

"Okay," Charlie said. "I was really, really ugly. Chicks hated me. Little kids cried when they saw me. I couldn't cope."

Karen crossed her arms. "And you still can't."

Charlie turned to face her and crossed his arms back, his expression guarded.

"If I can cope, so can you."

Charlie didn't seem to have an answer for that. After a pause, he resorted to, "Fuck you."

"Been there," Karen said. "Done that."

For a moment, Karen thought Charlie would storm out of the room, but all he did was laugh.

Erica's mother's house looked nothing like her mother's house. For one thing, there was no wheelchair ramp. For another, it was considerably more upscale.

Charlie shivered in the driver's seat. "Are you sure you want to do this?"

Karen said nothing for a while. She didn't know what to say. Erica was dead and there was nothing she could do to bring her back. It was so unfair that Erica had to die so she could live.

Finally, she said, "I just wanted to see the house."

"We should go before they come out to talk to us," Charlie said.

Yes, that would probably be bad. "Okay."

Charlie started the car. He drove back the way they'd come, towards the highway. "I almost told someone you were my girlfriend."

Karen snickered. "You could do worse."

Charlie laughed. "Yeah." They merged onto the highway. "I didn't want to go out cruising for chicks. My friend asked me why, and I realized... I'd rather have dinner with you."

"I thought you were too fucked up for a relationship."

"I am," Charlie said, "but I think I'm getting better."

Karen said nothing. She just looked over at Charlie and watched his face.

"Maybe it's the therapy," he said. "Maybe it's the Wellbutrin. But I think the reason I have nothing to prove to myself any more is you."

Karen didn't know what to say to that. This was what she wanted back in the chair. Finally, she said, "I'll cook."

Underworld

Dion tucked his computer science textbook and his Book of Shadows into his backpack, dropped it onto the floor at the foot of his bed, and launched World of Warcraft. He selected his realm: Earthen Ring. He was number eighty in the queue. Expected wait time: twenty minutes. Stupid server. He glanced over at the wilted plant on the windowsill and waved his wand at it, and it perked up.

His mother wandered into the room, wearing a gold lamé evening dress and hose without shoes, and he hid his wand behind his back. He made no attempt, however, to hide the glass of wine on the desk next to the computer. As long as he didn't get shit-faced, she had no problem with it.

She said, "Honey, have you seen my rhinestone earrings?" She walked over to his dresser and opened his jewelry box and looked inside, but Dion knew it didn't have any rhinestones in it. Just some pentagrams and crystals. "Be careful, baby," his mother said, picking up the pentagram. "You don't want to attract the wrong kind of attention."

Blah blah, people will think you're crazy blah, like there were no Wiccans in college. "You left them on the bathroom sink, so I put them in the medicine chest," he said. "I didn't want them to fall down the drain and get lost."

She dropped the pentagram back into the jewelry box. "Where would I be without my little man?" She walked over and kissed him on the cheek. Then she left, fancy dress rustling as she headed out the door.

Dion groaned. He was nineteen years old and six foot one; he was hardly his mother's little man. "You're welcome!" He could hear her chuckling in the other room. He glanced down at his computer console again. His position in the queue was now seventy-seven. "I'm not going to have to come rescue you again, am I?"

"Oh, hell no," his mother said, appearing in the doorway. Her makeup was impeccable, her dress was elegant, her rhinestones sparkled, and she was pinning a corsage to her chest. "I used to date him back when you were a baby. Mr. Kataibates is pure class. You should see what he drives! He has a gorgeous silver..."

"I don't care what he drives," Dion said. "I care that he treats my Mama right."

"I'll be fine, baby," she said. "Like my mama always said—it's as easy to fall in love with a rich man as it is a poor man." She winked at him. "Don't wait up, now."

Dion groaned again and threw a Darth Maul beanie baby at her. He heard the front door close and pulled out his wand. He murmured a spell and his position in the queue went from seventy-four to two. He put down his wand and grinned. He wasn't the best wizard in the world, but computers were easy. He was pretty good with plants and shapeshifting, too, which was why he played a druid. They were good at plants and shapeshifting, too.

He wondered again what his father was like—he'd clearly gotten his magical abilities from him, not his mother. But Mom wasn't talking.

He was awakened by Sir Mix-A-Lot announcing that he liked big butts and he could not lie. For a moment he thought it was just a crazy dream about rappers in his bedroom, but then he realized it was his cell phone. He rolled over and groped for his phone in the dark, knocking it off the nightstand and onto the floor. He scrambled and answered, "Hello?" and was surprised by how scratchy and incoherent his voice sounded, even to him.

"Baby, I'm so sorry to call you so late." His mother. "I'm so sorry, but I need you to come pick me up right away."

Dion sat up. "Mom?" There was a sliver of light from the streetlight coming in between the bedroom curtains forming a line of visibility over to his computer. He threw a book at the desk to jiggle the mouse and the screen lit up.

"I'm in the ladies room in the lobby of the Four Seasons hotel and I'm afraid to come out. I'll explain when you get here. Oh, shit, I think he's coming." She hung up.

Dion sighed, then scrambled out of bed by the light of the computer screen. Part of him thought that he should just leave his mother there; she kept getting into these messes, and it wasn't fair of her to expect her son to get her out all the time. He turned on the bedroom light and hissed at the brightness hitting his eyes, then grabbed his jeans and the first t-shirt he could find—the one that read "you are dumb" in binary—and threw them on. He pulled on his socks and sneakers, then crossed the room for his jewelry box and his pentagram.

Then he went into his mother's room and opened her Bible, which was where she kept her "mad money," and grabbed three hundred dollars in case he needed to bail her out or something. He grabbed his wand, wallet, and cell phone off his nightstand and stuffed them into his back pockets. There was a mirror over his dresser and he scowled at his reflection. He looked like a gangly teenager whose mother woke him up for a ride at...

The clock said 4 in the morning.

He swore and stormed out to his car, a cherry red 1984 Chevy Caprice. It was older than he was, but it had some serious juice. He hoped he wouldn't have to kick some old man ass. His mother tended to like rich pricks with expensive lawyers. He wondered if his father was a rich prick with an expensive lawyer. A rich wizard prick with an expensive lawyer. He snarled.

When he arrived at the Four Seasons hotel, there was a chill in the air but he had his irritation to keep him warm. Especially when the doorman—a thin, pimply white guy in an ill-fitting suit—watched him like a hawk and the women leaving clutched their purses closer as he walked by. Please. He knew for a fact that black people had been to the Four Seasons before. He resisted the urge to roll his eyes at them and figured his shirt said it all. The lobby was all marble and fancy wood and rugs and people in expensive clothes with a lot of jewelry. He walked over to the door marked 'Ladies' and was about to knock when a gorgeous, regal Greek woman came out. She was maybe forty and had dark curly hair piled up on her head and big, gorgeous, intense brown eyes. She wore understated makeup, a little royal blue dress, and pearls. She had a hair comb with peacock feathers on it. She was totally hot and probably had no use for a skinny, teenaged gamer geek. She turned back towards the door and said, "I believe your son is here." Maybe she was a friend of his mom's.

Dion's mother peeked around the woman, then rushed out and grabbed him by the arm. "Let's go."

"See you later, Semele," the woman in blue said.

"Not if I see you first," Dion's mom muttered. On second thought, maybe she wasn't a friend of his mom's.

As they were headed out the door, Dion asked his mother, "Who was that?"

"Mrs. Kataibates," his mother whispered.

"Mama!" He stopped and stared at her. He looked back at the woman in blue, who crossed her arms and smirked at him in a way that made him grab his mother's arm and hurry her towards the door.

"I didn't know he was married," his mother said.

Bullshit. How long had she known this guy? He was nineteen years old and she used to date Kataibates when he was a baby. Either Kataibates was a really good liar or his Mom... He didn't like either train of thought, but he liked the latter less.

There was a Greek man dressed entirely in black—black turtleneck, black jeans, black leather jacket—waiting next to Dion's car. There was something about him, a supernatural quality, something more frightening than just Greek mafia. "I'm afraid you'll have to come with me, Mel."

Dion's mother cowered behind him. Dion pulled out his wand and pointed it at the man. "Leave her alone!" A silvery glow came out of the wand and headed towards the man, but he seemed to have a protective shield around him. Well. That, and hexes weren't really his forte.

The man laughed. "Little boy, do you have any idea who I am?"

Dion shook his head.

"The name is Thanatos," the man said. He pulled something out of his pocket and everything went dark.

Dion woke up cold with a damp back and the doorman leaning over him. "Welcome back, kid." The ground smelled like motor oil.

Dion sat up. "Mama?"

"Gone," the doorman said. He handed Dion one of his mother's earrings and the corsage. Up close, Dion could tell the doorman's suit wasn't particularly well made. Well, he supposed it was a uniform of sorts.

"Did you call the police?" Dion asked.

The doorman laughed but there was no humor in it. "No, I value my life. That guy's Greek mafia, and those guys are untouchable. Olympians. Sorry, kid."

Dion scrambled to his feet. "Which way did they go?"

"Forget it. Your mother's in a shallow grave right about now. Go home." He looked at Dion's car and said, "I'll call you a cab."

Dion looked over at his car and started to swear. That dick Thanatos had slashed his tires.

He grabbed the doorman's arm. "Which way did they go?"

The doorman shook his head, pulled his arm free, and walked away. Dion flipped him the bird behind his back. His mother might be a... a... the other woman, but she loved him and he loved her.

He tucked the earring into his pocket and hung the corsage like a pendulum. "Which way did they go?"

The corsage pulled to the right.

The doorman whistled. He turned, and the doorman was waving him over to a cab. He ran and climbed into the back seat. The cab looked clean but it smelled like coffee and salami.

"Where to?" the cab driver asked. He was an old man in a fisherman's sweater with flashing pale-blue eyes.

"That way," Dion said, pointing in the direction the corsage pointed.

The old man gave him and the corsage pendulum an appraising look. "It's extra if I cross the river."

Dion realized that no one was reacting to him practicing magic. He didn't know if that was good or bad. Maybe the cab driver was "the wrong kind of attention." Thanatos sure as hell was. Either way, it was too late to worry about it now.

They followed the corsage pendulum across the river and through scary, half-deserted streets with boarded-up windows and shambling bums who threw empty bottles at the cab as he passed. They finally found himself in an abandoned warehouse. He got out of the cab. "Wait for me."

"It'll cost extra," the man said. "In advance."

Dion nodded and handed the man a hundred-dollar bill, making sure he saw that he had more where that came from. He opened the warehouse door. It was dark and dirty and smelled musty. There were concrete stairs leading down and voices. At the bottom of the stairs, a dog growled. Dion wished he'd remembered the beef jerky he had in his backpack for when he didn't have time for lunch, because he wasn't any good at dogs at all. But the corsage insisted his mother was down there, so he pulled out his wand and decided to play Warcraft druid. "Root!" he said, and vines rose up and tied up the dog, who was understandably confused by the whole thing. Since that worked, he decided to try to become a leopard. His beard stubble became kitty whiskers and he dropped to all fours. He would have thought it would hurt, but instead he felt more athletic. And really hairy. Light became brighter, colors dimmer, edges less distinct. The dog whimpered. Dion thought he smelled something nasty—the dog, gross! No wonder cats hated dogs. He walked past the dog, who looked well and truly freaked out.

He couldn't believe it worked! So freaking cool! He changed back and did an insulting little touchdown dance. The dog lunged at him, vines gone, teeth towards his face, snarling and pulling at the end of its chain. Dion leapt back and almost fell, but he caught himself just in time.

He crossed over a footbridge—well, more of a concrete plank over a gutter—and up another flight of concrete stairs. His mother was there, lying on the floor, her pretty dress covered with blood and dirt and her face bruised and swollen. He thought she was dead at first, but then she let out a tiny little sob and he knew she'd seen him. She didn't move, though, not even when Thanatos kicked her. He swallowed the salty fluid that welled up in his mouth—a prelude to vomiting, which would reduce his intimidation factor, such as it was—clenched his fists and sized up the other people in the room.

Aside from Thanatos, there was a man and a young, tall, willowy, sad-eyed brunette. The man had long, silky black hair—almost prettier than the woman's—and was wearing a silk suit and a diamond ring. He was younger than Mrs. Kataibates, but...

"Are you Kataibates?" Dion asked the man.

The man in the silk suit laughed a mirthless bark of a laugh. "Ordinarily I'd be flattered, but since I've just learned that my brother-in-law has once again failed to keep it in his pants..." He shook his head. "You should go now. I have many guests and most of them are not permitted to leave."

"What the hell?" Thanatos said, starting towards Dion.

"Wait!" the tall brunette said, grabbing Thanatos' arm. "You can't kill him."

"Why not?"

"Because," the brunette said, "he's Kataibates' kid."

Oh, shit. His father *was* a rich wizard prick. A rich Greek mafia wizard prick, who probably had an army of expensive lawyers. And an angry wife. Dion resisted the urge to swear. He looked over at his mother, but she didn't move or look at him.

Thanatos looked over at the man in the silk suit. "Is this true, Polydektes?"

The man in the silk suit raised an eyebrow at Thanatos. The coldness of his stare made Dion shiver and it wasn't even directed at him.

Thanatos blinked. "Mister Polydektes. Sir."

Mr. Polydektes appeared unmollified.

"And don't think for a moment that Kataibates doesn't know it," the brunette continued. "He's been paying child support for years—under the table, of course, so his wife wouldn't find out."

Dion thought of the hundred-dollar bills in his pocket and winced. No one seemed to notice.

"Well, she found out," Polydektes said. "And I'm not going to just let the bitch go. I owe it to my sister to look out for her interests, and if this chick has no respect for the marital vows... well, that's her funeral."

"Your sister can take care of herself, honey," the brunette said.

"It's a matter of loyalty."

The woman rolled her eyes, and Polydektes pulled her closer and gave her a peck on the cheek. It was her turn to look unmollified.

"They made my sister cry," Polydektes said, his voice surprisingly soft.

Dion considered that Mrs. Kataibates hadn't been crying when he saw her, but said nothing.

"Maybe," Thanatos said, "if it was supposed to be all hush-hush, he shouldn't have taken her to the Four Seasons."

"I'm not leaving without my mother," Dion said. "So you're going to have to either kill me or hand her over."

Polydektes rolled his eyes. "Oh, go away, kid. You're bothering the grown-ups."

"I'll tell you what," Dion said. "If I can kick his ass"—he pointed at Thanatos—"I get to walk out of here with my mom. Deal?"

Polydektes laughed, but it wasn't a cheerful sound. "It's up to you, Persephone."

The brunette chewed her lip a little. Dion handed her the corsage with a deep bow.

"Deal," she said. She pulled a black ribbon out of her hair and used it to the corsage to her wrist. "Why don't you bring me flowers any more?"

Polydektes leaned over and whispered something in Persephone's ear that made her smile.

Dion gave Thanatos a long, appraising look. Thanatos smirked back at him. He clearly didn't have the magical chops to fight this guy with spells, but Thanatos hurt his mother.

He threw himself onto Thanatos in a flying tackle, punching wildly and shrieking in rage. Thanatos was clearly not expecting that and was pulling his punches. Apparently he didn't want to hurt Kataibates' son.

Dion didn't pull his punches. He kept hitting until his hands were covered with blood, and finally Thanatos turned on him, his eyes icy. Dion felt his limbs grow cold and numb.

"Root!" Dion said, and vines sprouted up out of the earth and twined around Thanatos. Grape vines with thick, lush bunches of grapes covering Thanatos' shoulders and eyes. Thanatos blinked and looked around, and Dion felt his limbs tingle with the blood rushing back to them. He turned into a leopard and lunged for Thanatos' throat. Blood mingled with the sweet taste of grapes in his mouth, rich and intoxicating. He shook Thanatos out like a dishrag, then tossed him aside and pounced again. He tore at Thanatos' limbs and chest, vaguely aware of screams.

"Stop," Polydektes said.

Dion ignored him, planting a paw on Thanatos' chest and gnawing a limb off. And then Persephone was there, placing a hand on his chest. He was going to growl at her, but he was distracted by her sad eyes. They were deep and dark, like the earth.

She reached up a hand and stroked his head, and he leaned into her touch. "It's all right. Everything will be all right."

"Damn," Polydektes said and shook his head. "You really are my brother-in-law's kid. You got his temper, that's for sure."

Dion ran over to his mother, turning back into a human. He picked her up and she weakly wrapped her arms around his neck, like a child. "We'll be going now."

Thanatos whimpered, and Polydektes leaned over and casually pressed Thanatos' arm back into its socket like he was made of clay. Then he looked up at Dion, his eyes unreadable. "That would be wise, yes."

Dion took a step backwards, then turned and carried his mother as fast as he could. He didn't look to see if anyone was following him.

When they got to the dog, Dion said, "I just kicked Thanatos' ass. You don't want to fuck with me, dog. In the name of Hecate, down." The dog dropped onto his stomach, growling, but he let them by. He got into the taxi, his mother on his lap, and handed the driver another hundred. It was covered with blood, and he didn't know whether it was Thanatos' blood or his mother's. The driver raised an eyebrow and started the car.

Dion asked his mother, "He's my dad?"

His mother's voice was a whisper. "He told me he was divorced. I believed him."

Dion wasn't sure he believed her, but it didn't matter. She was his mother. He had her back.

Dion looked up from his computer science textbook—stateless firewalls—as his mother swept into the room. She was wearing a white lace blouse and a flowered skirt. She pirouetted. "What do you think?"

His heart sank. "You have a date?"

"Yes, with the nice man who owns the bookstore on the corner," she said. "I don't expect to be out too late."

"Okay," he said, because there wasn't anything else to say. She left. He tried to finish his reading, but he was distracted. Who knew what kind of asshole the bookstore guy was? Who knew what other rich assholes his mother might get involved with?

It occurred to him that he apparently had an in with a very rich, very powerful, very dangerous asshole. One who could be an insurance policy against anyone else doing his mother wrong.

So he Googled up Kataibates. There was a phone number for Kataibates Enterprises, which he dialed.

"Kataibates Enterprises," a perky receptionist said. He could almost hear her smacking gum in the background and wondered if she was his age.

"Yes, I'd like to speak to Mr. Kataibates."

"May I ask who's calling?" she asked.

"His son."

Her voice took on a suspicious tone. "Which one?"

"The illegitimate one."

"Which one?" the receptionist asked, her tone dry.

"Dion," he said.

"I'll... tell him you're on the line." She'd heard of him? Really?

There was a pause, and then an older man picked up. "This is Kataibates." He hesitated, and when he spoke again, his voice sounded uncertain—almost vulnerable. "Dion?"

"You and I need to talk," Dion said, "about protection for my mother."

About the Author

Katherine Villyard was born in Dallas, Texas. Her father was civilian support for the military, so she moved every two years and attended four different high schools. The most exotic one to US readers will probably be Kaiserslautern American High School in Germany, but her favorite was Arts Magnet High School at Booker T. Washington in Dallas, where she studied theater. She also went through a phase where she wore a lot of white dresses and sat in windowsills writing (bad) poetry—what she called her "Emily Dickinson phase."

Katherine's first short story, a tale of a clown in a balloon, was well received in First Grade and proudly displayed for the entire school to read. She wrote the odd short story in high school about such topics as forced conformity and parodies of horror movies.

Katherine's mother wanted her to major in Computer Science in college. Katherine has a Bachelor of Fine Arts degree in studio ceramics and weaving. She has two Master's degrees: one in Fine Arts and the other in Library Science. So, of course, Katherine went into Information Technology (Computer Science) after being "poached" by her University's Academic Computing department, where she worked as a student assistant while in grad school. She wrote websites for pay from 1995 to 2002.

She started writing again during the "dot bomb" crash. Following a trip to the unemployment office filled from wall to wall with unemployed software engineers and web developers, she spotted an online listing to write lesbian erotica for a hundred dollars and said to herself, "I can do that!" She wrote the story, sent it off... and never heard back. She wrote as a hobby for some time, but when friends started sending things out to be published, she jumped off that roof as well. (Insert disapproving Mom face here.) Her work has appeared in Escape Pod, Electric Velocipede, and Fantastic Stories of the Imagination.

Katherine is a former Microsoft MVP in Enterprise Security, a member of the Science Fiction and Fantasy Writers Association, and on the Broad Universe Motherboard. She has a tendency to develop nerdy fascinations and research binge. Previous topics include Pueblo pottery, Navajo weaving, Pre-Columbian art, Frida Kahlo, Percy and Mary Shelley, and Eleanor of Aquitaine. When she's not writing, working, or research binging, she's probably spoiling cats or playing The Sims.

Her greatest ambition is to rule the world.

Want to read another short story by me? You can get one here:

You can visit Katherine at her website at https://www.katherinevillyard.com, or follow her on Goodreads at https://www.goodreads.com/kmankiller. Katherine also has a Pinterest, where she collects pictures for her upcoming novel, and a YouTube, which is mostly silly cat videos.

Thanks for reading! If you enjoyed this book, please consider leaving a review at the place where you bought it.

Made in United States
Orlando, FL
30 October 2023

38377677R00117